The Golden Age
Torture Magic Novel 4.5 (49)

By Douglas Todt

First Edition (2022)

The Golden Age
Torture Magic Novel 4.5 (49)
By Douglas Todt

This season of Torture Magic is a little different. If you've been a reader of the Outcasts series, you don't have to read the TM series to enjoy the finale, or vice versa. But if you read both, it's more fun.

For readers of the Torture Magic series, series five will be back to the normal format (or close to it) in 2023.

All readers can enjoy the related book, the first appearance of the Cube, Las Vegas' newest superheroine. Shelby's series is set in the Ops world, but it does not *directly* tie-in with the Torture Magic series. Her book I consider 4.X (46) and falls between 4.2 and 4.3 of the regular series.

The Outcasts Path
Outcasts I – VII

The Intersection
Outcasts VIII / TM 4.0 "Merger"

Torture Magic Season Four
The Killer Inside (4.1)
Destination - Hell (4.2)
Survival of the Fittest (4.3)
No Ifs, Ands, or Butts (4.4)
The Golden Age (4.5)

Related Books
The Call Girl Superheroine (4X)

Chapter One
Tachyonic Physics 101
Sunday, June 27, 2021

Every joint Sam Grant had ached. Ever since he discovered he had rheumatoid arthritis (RA) in late 2020, his life had gone into the toilet. Today, the knees and shoulders were the problems, but the joints with pain rotated unpredictably over time, as did the pain. All of his joints burned today, and the pain was significant.

The one-time leader of field operations in Special Operations, the secret government division that dealt with the paranormal, Sam was now a semi-retired field agent, helping out where and when he could. He tried to help Ops when he could. But the last few weeks, the RA had gotten worse, so he spent his time either at his second home in Julian, outside San Diego, or visiting with his late first wife Bam's mom in Chicago.

Because of the RA, travel had become difficult at times, especially driving. He treated it with Humira, a bit risky because, in the Ops world, exposure to disease was pretty common. Ops was trying to balance his medication with the need to avoid tanking his immune system. On days like this, he felt it wasn't working.

Now fifty-three, Sam was slightly balding, his brown, curly hair fading to gray. He had brown eyes and a short, five-foot and eight-inch wiry frame. He also had a big nose that looked a bit like a vulture's beak.

Sam had joined Ops in 2005 after a stint with the NSA. Brought on board by Ops' long-time director, General Emerald Jon Jameson, Sam had basically taken over daily operations in 2014 when Jameson was fired or sent on secret missions, depending on the perception. He had met his wife, Bam Cartier-Grant, in 2007 while working for Ops, but she had been murdered by the torture magician Shanna McGruder in 2014.

Not long after that, he met Meredith Patience. And not long after that, they began a relationship.

Then she died.

In January of 2018, Sam took time off, and basically worked as a field agent while being unofficially retired. That led him in July 2020 to become ensnared by Amy Dayne and the Consortium's plot to put Dayne in as President in 2020 while posing as Shy Strong. Sam became Public Enemy Number One. Even though he had been fully exonerated a month earlier, he still kept a low profile.

Ops' battle with the alien Quotient on New Year's Day had ended with Sam in a coma, part of a complex scheme that also led him to subconsciously send a team to Hell to destroy it. Sam had awakened form the coma February 16. In April, he was part of the team that battled Jennifer Troxit in St. Louis. In that battle, Colin Ridgeway had been killed . . . well, his parallel world self had been killed . . . Ops could get confusing. At any rate, since then, Sam had not taken on any new assignments. The RA had been worse, and he was sure it was due to stress.

But Ops needed him now. They needed *everyone* after the torture magician (TM) David Morrison unleashed what he called a new Golden Age into the atmosphere in Tiera del Fuego.[1]

Morrison was one of six high-level paranormals that executed the spell. Torture magicians were paranormals that used the pain and adrenaline uniquely generated by torture to create paranormal power — usually telekinesis, but in Morrison and his allies' case, they had some other abilities. A near death experience (NDE) had left

---

[1] In our previous book, TM 4.4 "No Ifs, Ands, or Butts"

Morrison able to manipulate tachyons on a previously unseen scale as well as the ability to communicate, on a limited basis, with the dead.

Per his earlier call with Medina, Sam arrived at the University of California-San Diego, or UCSD as all the locals knew it, one of the most prestigious universities in the country. The sprawling campus in La Jolla had some of the most temperate weather in the country and was an idea place for learning. The finest minds worldwide came to UCSD.

So did plenty of visitors and third-party government organizations, hence Sam's visit for Special Ops. Sam wasn't paranormal himself, which wasn't atypical. Ops had about one hundred field agents but only 20-25 paranormals at any given time. Paranormals were rare, with perhaps one hundred on the entire planet.

During his time at Ops, Sam was stationed at a home in La Jolla, so he knew UCSD well. He had sold the home a little while back, not long after he quit in early 2018 right after Meredith died.

He planned to park in one of the campus parking structures, turning in slowly. The campus was beautiful and sprawling, but having been here several times, he had little trouble finding his way on the road. To his left were dorms that frankly looked better than most condo complexes in the area, mini-homes in a wooded area shaded from the bright sun by plenty of eucalyptus trees.

He drove up to level five and parked in the corner opposite the main walk of the campus, near the intersection. There were only a handful of cars on this level, given it was a Sunday in summer. He was certain he hadn't been followed.

Exiting, he looked around cautiously and approached the parking structure's elevator and walkway. He took the stairs, which were outside the structure, to the seventh and top level. Due to some interesting geography, this level was even with the walkway into the campus, as most of the parking garage was recessed.

The campus was wonderful and fairly quiet, the day being 72 degrees and sunny at eleven in the morning. Typical San Diego coastal

June weather, although the June gloom, in the form of ocean clouds, had cleared a little early, and the sun was bright.

He paused by a green Prius van parked near the short pedestrian bridge that led over a small access road that led to the main campus via the social studies building, a large building to the left of the walkway.

Casually, Sam wandered over and opened the passenger door.

Behind the wheel was Medina Kane.

About thirty, Medina was a pretty and charismatic young woman — all Kanes were charismatic — albeit very different from her older sister and Ops' superstar, Geneva. Medina was a little chunky around the waist, but generally hid that with fashionable clothes. Her blonde hair was now very curly, a marked change from her younger days when she kept it straight and long, but it was parted in the middle and flat on top, held back with hairpins. She had wide, bright blue eyes, and always wore a lot of mascara and make-up. Her blush was light pink, and her preferred lipstick was bright red.

She wore a royal blue skirt with a light pink blouse, white nylons, and white heels. Her purse was white, and her sunglasses had pink frames. She exited the Prius, then smiled and said, "You walk slow."

"Gee, thanks for building my spirits, boss. No wonder your sister says you're the most annoying person in the universe," said Sam, referring to Medina's older sister, Geneva, who had joined Ops at age eighteen in 2005 and was considered the premier field agent in the organization.

She clapped him on the shoulder. "Sorry."

"I know you're teasing. So was I . . . maybe," Sam said, giving her a wry smile.

"Well, I'm glad you made it," said Medina with a smile, and they kept walking. "Was the drive bad?"

"Not terrible. Julian's about forty-five minutes without traffic."

"What were you doing up there anyhow?"

Sam sighed. "Well, back in '17, when I was stationed in La Jolla, I bought a fixer-upper out there . . . I kind of left it behind when Meredith died. I guess I felt it was time to do something with it. I'm fixing up to have some sort of permanent residence, someplace warm, thanks to the arthritis." He shrugged. "With this arthritis, I can't go back home. Can't handle the winters." Sam was born and raised in Racine, Wisconsin.

"I see," she said, and having been raised in Maine, she knew what he meant about winters back East.

Meredith Patience had been Sam's lover after Bam passed. Their relationship had been complex and confusing, partly due to the age difference, but mostly due to Meredith's history of trauma. Everyone believed Meredith died in 2018 battling the TM avatar David Everett, but later it was found she was shunted to a parallel universe. She returned for just hours in 2020 before she was murdered by Calico Kelkirk in the raid on Storm Island.[2]

Medina wasn't heavily involved with Ops at the time, but she knew enough from talks with her sister to know she didn't want to get into *any* discussion about Sam and Meredith.

"I'm not much of a handyman," said Sam. "Even before I got RA. I haven't drilled a hole in my thumb or anything yet, though."

"Sometimes you have to try new things," she said diplomatically.

They exited and walked together to the campus. The buildings were tall, the walkways wide, the campus heavily lined with trees.

"This is a nice place," said Medina.

"it's one of the best universities in America, or so Bam used to tell me. It should be for what it costs."

Medina laughed. "Try going to Wellesley!"

"No, thanks," said Sam. "I'm a state school kind of guy."

Given it was a Sunday afternoon, the campus was generally quiet, but there were a dozen coeds scattered about, moving between the buildings, and two security people.

"There's our building," said Medina.

Sam nodded. They had walked left form the social studies building to find a building on the left marked super computers. The building itself was tall and brown, but there was an odd black tile structure

---

[2] In TM 5.4 "The Island the World Forgot"

adjacent to it, like universe-patterned bathroom tile. This was a special cooling unit for the supercomputer work being done inside.

Sam held the door for Medina, and they entered. It seemed dark and cold inside after being out in the sun. Medina took off her sunglasses and Sam squinted for a minute.

The lobby was large. There was a room index on a gold-plated panel next to the elevator. Medina checked it and said, "Here we come room 412."

They walked down the empty corridor, footsteps echoing.

"Have you worked with Dr. Tang?" Sam asked her as they rode upwards.

Medina shook her head. "No. She just came to our attention recently. She had been researching particle physics, but she stumbled on something odd, which got back to us at Ops. I gave her a blank check to research, because it's to do with probability clouds."

"Ah," said Sam.

Probability clouds were tachyonic events where the improbable became probable. They caused odd things, from the creation of the soul survivor Jennifer Saunders in 2004 to the bestowment of a higher-than-normal level of paranormal events, including manifestations. They were a major concern to Ops.

They reached the large office door for 412 and Medina knocked on it. "Dr. Tang, it's Medina Kane."

"Come in, it's open."

They entered to find Dr. Davina Tang, a mousey looking brunette aged thirty-one with her hair in a ponytail and gigantic glasses that made her look like a cartoon character looking out of a telescope. She wore a lab coat over black slacks with sneakers, and was very short, not taller than five two. She was sitting behind a very messy desk, backed into the corner, the blinds pulled and the room full of books and bizarre looking physics displays. The walls were covered in charts.

"Hi! Who's the hunk?" asked Davina when she saw Sam, clearly teasing.

"He's my, ah, personal assistant, Mr. Grant," said Medina quickly.

Sam stepped forward and shook Davina's hand. "Nice to meet you. Nice office."

She shrugged. "It gets me by. My problem today is I lost a fucking contact lens, so I'm wearing these god damn telescopic lenses. I feel like a fucking mole creature. Sit down and stay, gang."

They sat in two of the four black leather chairs scattered in the office. The plastic plant was dusty, and the floor had scuff marks. There wasn't much wall space visible.

Medina smiled and said, "We won't take much time. I've read the report you sent. Sam and I have some questions."

She made a gun out of her finger. "Shoot."

Medina said, "Your report stated that at the time of the incident last Sunday/Monday, depending on where one was standing, when that paranormal EMP flare went out, an *entirely new* particle was released into the atmosphere. Can you elaborate a bit?"

"I'm just her assistant, so it takes me a while to catch on," said Sam without the hint of a smile.

"Surrrrrrrrre." She clapped her hands. "What was created was something that has never been seen before. Never. Trust me, I consulted thousands of research facilities, but there's only about a dozen, including UCSD, that would be into this sort of shit. I'm calling it a QPC — a quantum probability cloud particle. But I have no idea what it does."

"Why use the term quantum?" asked Sam.

She looked at him, then looked at Medina. "You have other questions, boss?"

"Uh, well, several. You mentioned it's spreading through the atmosphere and have a bunch of graphs, but is the rate steady or fast? And how soon will we all be swimming in it? And what does it do?"

"It's an even rate, generally speaking. There's slight variances, which I can't explain, but overall it's less than a one percent variance. If the pace maintains itself, which isn't guaranteed but this far along is likely, the world will be covered from penguins to Santa Claus within 32 days."

Medina frowned. "From now or the inception date?"

"Inception date."

Sam cleared his throat and said, "So you haven't figured out what it does?"

"Nope. We're studying it, but each time we look at it, it appears to be something different," she said. Then she pointed at Sam. "Hence my clever name."

"How is that possible?" asked Medina.

Tang shrugged. "It's quantum physics."

Medina asked, "Doctor, what *is* Quantum Physics, in layman's terms? Because we each have college degrees, and despite that, we each have no clue what it is."

Tang smiled thinly. "It's just the study of the behavior of matter and energy at the microscopic level, smaller than that, really. Basically, laws governing macroscopic objects," and she tapped her desk, "like this thing do not function the same in small realms."

"Okay," said Medina uncertainly.

"The basic tenant is that observing something actually influences the physical processes taking place. Light waves act like particles, and particles act like waves. Matter moves from one spot to another without moving through intervening space."

"Sounds like the Justice League's old matter transporter," said Sam.

"Quantum tunnelling is the precise term," she said. "Information moves instantly across vast distances. At the core, the entire universe is actually a series of probabilities. But with larger objects, it breaks down. That's the Schrodinger's Cat experiment."

"I've heard of that as very famous, but never really sat down and looked at it," said Sam.

"Same," said Medina.

Davina laughed. "It's simple. The Schrödinger's cat experiment demonstrates the strange nature of quantum superposition." She made spooky noises and waved her hands like a witch. "A cat is placed in a box with a vial of poison, which will be automatically released if a radioactive particle decays. Radioactive decay is one of the probability-driven aspects of quantum physics. We can't say when a given particle will decay, we only know the *probability* of it decaying in a certain period. After some time has elapsed, an unobserved particle will be in a superposition of decayed and not decayed states. All that exists before measurement, meaning some lame-ass looking inside the box, is the *probabilities*. But since the life of the cat depends on the state of the particle, does this mean the poor, fucked-over cat is simultaneously dead and alive?

"In reality, it's impossible to witness the cat being both alive and dead – as soon as we look in the box, the cat will be in just one state. And the practicalities of the experiment don't even allow for this. For the detector to be able to release the poison it would have to interact with the particle, forcing it to be either decayed or not decayed."

"That gave me a headache," said Medina.

"It takes time to work through."

Sam frowned and rubbed his chin. "You're saying this particle could allow dual states of being at the same time?"

"I'm saying *it changes as its observed*," said Davina, her jovial manner gone. "That's the difficult studying the QPC. It's almost as if it's disguising itself deliberately. I've never seen anything like it, and its existence makes shit like Schrodinger's cat look like preschool physics."

Sam nodded. "I see."

"I wish I fucking did."

Medina smiled. "I have to say, you aren't quite like most physicists I've talked with."

She smiled. "I'm something called a multiple personality, have this thing called dissociative identity disorder. I survived a hurricane as a child and lay with corpses for days. I created alternate personalities. Right now, I'm Mary, the liaison for the inner core and the exterior world. Albert's the physicist." She rolled her eyes. "As you might have guessed."

"Well, you seem very well-adjusted," said Sam.

"I get by."

Medina slung her purse over her shoulder and said, "Well, thanks, doc. We'll keep in touch."

"Certainly. You know the way out?"

"Yes. Thanks."

They exited and began reversing the walk, speaking casually. There were a few people out and about, all co-ed types. Neither Sam nor Medina was worried they were being tailed or overheard.

Medina said grimly, "Thirty-two days. Basically, a month, and we've used up a week of that month already. That isn't much time."

"Well, we don't even know if we have *that* long," said Sam as they rounded a corner turning left for the parking lot. "Maybe they just want these QPCs over a specific area."

"I hadn't thought of that, but if so, why not just do the spell where they want to and get it to work immediately?"

Sam nodded. "Valid point. There could have been geographic restrictions, like this isn't a spell that could be performed in downtown Tokyo. But, well, I guess, since we're talking Consortium affiliated persons and knowing their primary goal is saving us all from global warming, global spread does fit." He paused. The Consortium was a band of governments, paranormals, and businesses seeking a stated objective of saving humanity from global warming. Their ends were fine, but their means generally involved millions or billions of innocent casualties. Ops had stopped two of their plans in 2020, but Morrison's plan looked dangerously close to success now. "There's still nothing to say the spread ratio will remain where it is now. We know absolutely nothing about this."

"Yeah. It's how I feel when you use comic book references," she joked. "And I don't think we'll ever find them again. Morrison, Morgana, they've closed up shop."

"Oh, we don't have to *find* them," said Sam. "We know where they'll go now. With Valeria involved, there's only one place that will be safe."

"Ah. Glickstenstein."

"Yep. It's her country. No, the more important factor is to figure out what this is all about, because we can't stop it by just ringing on the front doorbell or flying there and beating the shit out of them, as fun as that might be. We'll have to have a counter-channeling effort to stop them, but we're in the dark as to how they did this in the first place."

They had reached the parking garage. Medina used her remote to open the car and sighed. "That opens a lot of doors, Sam. What is the intention of the particles? What if they make a mistake? How did they do this the first time? Is there a counter-spell, and if so, how do we trigger it?"

They got inside the car. Medina started it. The radio came on, hooked to Medina's Bluetooth, playing Lady Gaga.

As she pulled into traffic, Medina added, "It's not like we can just call and ask them. No one knows about this shit."

"True, but they had help to set up shop in Tierra del Fuego. So, we need to pressure anyone who helped them with *that*. I'm sure others inside the Consortium were involved."

"That sounds like a Hail Mary."

"It pretty much is. At least we have the doc."

"Forget something?" asked Davina as she shouted at the door in response to the knocking. "It's still open."

The door opened.

And Dr. Tang was dead six seconds later.

Chapter Two
The Hunt
Monday, June 28, 2021

"Tang is dead," said Medina glumly as Sam entered the small cafeteria on the same floor as Medina's office at Special Operations headquarters in Las Vegas the next day.

Sam was stunned. He stopped in the middle of the floor and said, "What?"

Medina pointed a finger gun at her temple and pulled the trigger. "Just like that."

Sam joined her at a small, round table, sat in a white plastic chair, and said, "Damn."

Founded in 1974 by then Director General Jameson, the center was more like a college campus than a government operation. It consisted of office buildings, but also long-term residential units and the most sophisticated medical units for treatment of long-term torture survivors in the country. It had become the foremost treatment center for the traumatized in the nation. Ops often had to aid victims of torture magic.

Medina nodded with sadness. She wore a white blouse, red pants, white heels, and a frown. Sam wore a purple Milwaukee Brewers' T-shirt and white shorts with ancient white sneakers.

"I just heard about thirty minutes ago," said Medina, sipping a coffee. "I was up until eleven or so doing reports and selling off some property." She snapped her fingers. "We sold that warehouse in Wichita Falls where those vampires were nested for 90 grand."

"Good work."

She smiled. But then she immediately frowned. "I liked Doctor Tang, and she died because of us."

"Unlikely. No one knew we were there. Someone else probably got wind of her research and decided to shut her up. There's nothing we can do for her except make her sacrifice count," said Sam.

"I don't feel that way. I feel like shit," said Medina.

"Well, so do I. But when you lead field ops, innocent people pay for the decision. You should feel bad and should feel guilty and should feel like you failed. But those feelings are for when you're lying in bed at night, not when you are sitting in headquarters with a chance to do something about it. Who else knows?"

"The WSA, of course. And Radar. No one else yet. Obviously, none of the field agents knew her, but I figured Radar could research her work."

Sam nodded. "Then let's go to your office and talk to him."

"I like what you've done with this office," said Sam as they entered. "Little Jack's old office looked like the inside of a wristwatch!"

"Thanks," she said. The office was her design. There was a long, glass desk that had computer screens built into it, a matching glass chair, and an image of a black curtain that she could trigger when she wanted to sit with a little privacy. The carpet was lush blue and white, while the walls were a matching royal blue and the trim white. The windows showing the mountains east of Vegas were unchanged from Little Jack's tenure. But the entire area behind the desk was different. Now there was a picture of a beautiful ski slope in Switzerland. A grandfather clock was centered on the wall, the flags of Nevada and the United States to the left and right respectively. The sun shone brightly through the windows.

The far walls had eight television screens on each side wall, while the near wall was all pictures of Geneva and her family, the Kanes, who were to Ops what the Kennedys were to Democrats. There was a large, black leather sofa, several white leather chairs, and the doors worked remotely from the desk.

As Medina sat behind her desk and prepared to cue Radar on the screen behind her, Sam said, "Any popcorn?"

"No," said Medina, clearly still bothered by Tang's death.

Sam recognized this. "I'm sorry, Medina. I know this upsets you, and I'm not joking to be insensitive. It's my defense mechanism."

She forced a smile. "Thanks, Sam."

Radar suddenly appeared on the screen. John Patience was Meredith's uncle. Soon after Zenith killed John's brother, Meredith's father, John attacked Zenith. He got his ass kicked and portaled to the then parallel world where Jennifer Saunders was fighting against a world already dominated by Zenith. Radar was burning alive and dying. However, the resistance in the parallel world saved him.

During 2020, Radar returned to his native Earth, our Earth, with some of Ops' team. Since then, he had been working out of the insurance company run by former TMs in Germany. The TMs had been killed in the 2020 battles, but the insurance company was doing just fine.

The six existing robot Radars were all tall and gaunt with curly gray hair, a very weathered face, a thick mustache, and haunted blue eyes. They were designed to allow him to pass as completely human, hence they each cost about six billion dollars. To one who didn't know Radar, the robots appeared to be a man in his late forties, maybe 50, but he was in good condition. This robot wore a tight-fighting blue dress shirt that hugged his biceps, no tie, black pants, and dress shoes that had sneaker-shoe soles. With the light behind him, he looked like a sinister bank robber. A very tall man, he was at least six feet and five inches tall. Currently, he wore a black T-shirt with a photo print of Willie Nelson and jeans. He was obviously sitting in a car in a parking structure somewhere.

"Kane, Grant, Radar four here."

"Where is here?" asked Sam.

Radar chuckled. "I'm in a parking garage at the UCSD extension in San Diego. Sam, you'd know it, the one you can see from the 805."

"Yeah," said Sam.

"Anyhow, I got your alert on Tang, Medina. I'm sorry, really, but it may have exposed something important. I didn't figure the Consortium would send just any dickwad to off someone like Tang. They didn't. They sent one of their best. I'll share my screen."

A woman appeared on screen.

"A bit chubby, but still pretty good looking. Who is she?" asked Sam.

"Maureen Hollander, born in the Detroit area, Troy to be specific, went to high school in Tucson, Arizona and graduated with a degree in poly-sci from Arizona State. She's been a Society member since she turned 18 in 2003."

"Great. Who *is* she? I've never heard of her," said Sam.

"Me either," said Medina.

Sam and Medina studied the woman. She was a pretty woman, probably mid-thirties (unless the photo was a glamour, which TMs could use to make their appearance older or younger, the latter usually the case). She had a couple of wrinkles on an otherwise attractive face. Her eyes were wide and brown, and she had round cheeks. Her lips were pink, her face freckled, and she was well tanned. Her hair was blonde and rather messy, something like long and curly with an odd cut in the front. Her butt and legs were heavy, clearly a woman that had been in shape but time in the office had provided padding. But she was still attractive, with her legs being her best feature. The surveillance shot was outside an ATM. She wore a red, professional skirt with a flower print blouse, white hose, and red heels. On her wrists were two gold bracelets, one on each arm.

"I know you haven't. Neither had I until a few hours ago," said Radar with a grin.

Medina said irritably, "Well, spill the beans."

"Sorry. I just . . . okay, we gotta talk about this seriously and carefully, because if I've read my info right . . . this chick . . . may well be the woman behind the spell that stripped Chase of her ability to channel back in '19."

Sam glared and balled his fist. Medina said, "That . . . boy, *that's* some news."

"No shit," snarled Sam.

On February 24, 2019, Ops' veteran paranormal Chase Meridian was ambushed in a General Dynamics building near Costco in the San Diego suburb of Poway. A TM they later discovered to be Harmony Young used a spell to disrupt Chase's aura and remove her ability to channel. The power was taken by Young, but the main known effect was to cripple Chase. She went from being one of Ops' most powerful channelers to non-paranormal. A year later she was kidnapped and tortured, developing Stockholm syndrome and moving to France, where she was to this day.

"I can't say for sure she is. Like Kenny Rogers would say, you gotta know when to hold 'em and when to fold 'em, and right now I'd play that hand. It fits a few scenarios and some timelines on her I created," said Radar.

"I always wondered how Harmony pulled off that channeling trick," said Sam thoughtfully, "I mean, it didn't seem to fit her personality. From what Kahlia, bless her, relayed of their fight and from what I saw of Young when she ambushed me and Jameson in Arizona last year, Young didn't strike me as the type to be subtle enough to arrange all that. She was the foot soldier."

"I'd guess, yeah," said Radar.

"How did you get to her? Hollander, I mean," asked Sam.

He laughed. "For a change, it was pretty simple. Tang was killed on a Sunday, so it was pretty quiet on campus. They used something to kill the cameras, but that basically told me *when* Tang was killed. You didn't beat her by much. Anyhow, knowing that time, I was able to access cameras in the parking lots. I ran all the cars, easy for a robot of my abilities, and found a white '17 Camry registered to an outfit called Mark Two. That's a Consortium front. They do sham defense contracts to get facilities to use, and once such sham contract is with . . . wait for it . . . General Dynamics."

"Damn," said Sam, snapping his fingers. "General Dynamics is where Harmony ambushed Chase back in the day."

"Bingo. Anyhow, I got a good facial print from the parking lot camera of the woman getting into the car, and Ops' facial recognition software took it from there. Hollander is in the database from a Society meeting security scan I hacked in Germany."

"Well, we have our link," said Sam.

Medina shook her head. "You sure? Didn't Little Jack and company turn GD inside and out after Chase was ambushed?" Medina called up the files on computer built into the desk. "I mean, that's what it seems like on these reports to me."

Radar said, "Don't worry, kid. I can assimilate knowledge a bazillion times faster than you can read it."

Medina smiled. "Show-off."

"You bet. Let's see . . . yeah, so Hollander was never identified. The building Chase was ambushed in was a pure GD building. What's interesting is Mark Two signed a contract a few days *later*. They did this knowing they could come in as Mark Two and cover it up, and more importantly have an idea spot to experiment, I'd guess. I mean, who would search there after it was completely searched when Chase was attacked?"

"Fuckers," said Sam. "Chase was one of the first people Bam and I met and brought aboard at Ops.[3] She was a friend, not just an agent, and the person she was is . . . I want a piece of this. I owe them professionally and I owe them personally."

"Of course," said Medina. "But the question is, where is she *now*? Did they pick her to kill Tang because she's local?"

"Looks that way. She was in a DUI arrest ten days ago just about a mile east of the General Dynamics plant, the one on Kirkham off Scripps Poway Parkway, you know, the one where Chase was ambushed back in the day. They might have given her the field work as a way to slap her wrist, or she might just be a good killer. The latter I doubt, though, because we haven't run across her before."

---

[3] Way back in TM 1.4 "Shooting Straight at the Cape" in 2008

"Well, if she got a DUI, she's obviously hanging around. Now *that's* interesting," said Sam. "She's probably active in something there right now with this Mark Two corporation."

"I'd say so. I can poke around Consortium files, but Mark Two is high up. I'd rather not risk possibly alerting them."

"I agree," said Medina.

"I'm pretty excited," said Radar. "We never figured out exactly why Chase was picked, why that time, why that location, a lot of things. It gives one time to pause for thought . . . to make one wish he was a country and western singer and not a robot."

Sam laughed. "I've heard you sing. It's good you're a robot."

"Ah, you're an asshole, Grant," said Radar with a laugh. "Oh, I've contacted Shank, but the WSA never dealt with GD. So, we're somewhat on loose footing here."

Sam shrugged. "We could just show up and beat the shit out of her and see if that rattles her."

Medina shook her head. "Naw, we're too classy for that, Sam, and I have a better idea. Here's the plan."

Chapter Three
Infiltration
Friday, July 2, 2021

"Got weekend plans, Nicole?" asked playwright and stage guru David Peters on the evening of Thursday, July 1.

Nicole arched her eyebrows and wink with mock sexual suggestion. "Got plans for me?"

He laughed. "Nope. We all need the weekend off. We're working hard and ready for opening. The technical rehearsal will be the tenth. I think a break for everyone would be good."

"Actually, I did have plans to head back to LA and check on my condo and see old friends, if that's cool."

"I'm cool with everything you do," said Peters. "After all, you're the star."

Nicole Smith smiled. Twenty-four-years-old, Nicole wasn't extraordinarily pretty, but she was attractive. Average height and weight, her main asset was her face, which had the profile of a model. Her lips were ruby red, her skin fair and perfect, her eyes a brilliant shade of bright blue. Her hair was long, wavy, and jet black, running over her shoulders and down her back, with wide-cut bangs that ended just above her eyebrows in front.

Her voice was sometimes soft and sometimes throaty — an actress, she knew how to change her appearance and manner to get her point across. Physically, she stayed in shape with CrossFit workouts, but often she did them at home online. And while her features were average, she knew how to accent them to make them appear more favorable.

Nicole was wearing grape purple yoga pants and a yellow top, standing with her hands on her hips at the front of the stage to lean down and talk to Peters, the director, writer, and producer of the play for which Nicole was destined to be the star and have the lead female role. Behind her, a few of the troupe were still discussing aspects of certain scenes.

She nodded at the clock. "It's four. You mind if I drop off now? I have a flight out, actually, an overnight so I can have the full four days with the holiday. I want to see some friends."

"Sure. Be safe."

Nicole winked and blew him a kiss. Then she turned to a couple other members of the troupe, Tina and Mona. "Hey, girlfriends, I'm headed west for a few days. You gonna survive without me?"

"Getting drunk and getting laid will take care of that," said Tina, a curly haired blonde.

"I'm with here," agreed Mona.

Nicole laughed. "Can't beat that."

As she exited the theatre into a very hot evening in the Chicago southern suburb of Bolingbrook, where Nicole was part of a huge relaunch of entertainment that included a new theatre. Their play would open July 17, kind of an odd opening date as stage plays usually had fall or autumn openings, but delays in construction had pushed things back a few months. She shaded her eyes and found her car, a blue 2018 Nissan Versa. She got in and paused, rubbing her neck, just taking a moment to reflect on things as birds and bugs flew by.

Nicole *really was* spending the weekend with Ops, per Medina's texted request on Tuesday. Nicole agreed to help with going into GD undercover, knowing that Ops was still looking for Sunset and Morgana and the rest of the team that had executed the spell in Tierra de Fuego. She wanted to make sure Medina was still actively trying to find the two women torture magicians.

Sunset and Morgana were the TM daughter and mother team that had wrecked Nicole's life years ago, poisoning her father and making it appear he'd had a heart attack. When Nicole was a freshman at USC, she learned about this. She'd gone after whoever killed her father, only to be tossed off a roof in Anaheim by his TM acolyte agent, which caused her to manifest her channeling.

She then spent years hunting down her father's killers, who she discovered to be Sunset and Morgana. Her mother died of a true illness, and she lost her BFF and roommate, Audrey, to a rare disease during that time. After that, Nicole stepped up her quest for vengeance, taking a role undercover at the snuff film production company where Sunset and Morgana made the films. Nicole posed as a stupid, drug addict actress and TM acolyte.

That cost her dearly. During her infiltration into Sunset and Morgana's operation, she murdered a fellow actress, Tabitha. Sure, she risked reprisal if she didn't . . . but on a certain level, she had wanted to kill Tabitha, to give her freedom from her shitty life, but also because Nicole just was angry at her for putting her in such a position and angry she had to take care of it.

Nicole learned this in Hell while helping Sam Grant and the team save Earth from the Horal earlier in the year. She'd repressed the memory at the time it happened, December of 2017.

She hadn't yet fully processed her guilt and emotions. She was getting better, but Tabitha's death wasn't something she could ever talk about with anyone at Ops. She had told Medina in what she now feared might have been a moment of weakness. No one else would ever know.

No one.

"Got big plans, fella?" asked Dr. Regina Smith on Friday, July 2, 2021, though Regina was otherwise known as Ops' field agent *Nicole Smith*, as she approached the guarded entrance of General Dynamics' westernmost building on Kirkham Way in the San Diego suburb of Poway. They were about three buildings and half a mile east of the building near Costco where Chase had been ambushed in 2019.

"No, ma'am."

"Too bad. It should be a nice weekend. Thanks."

She walked inside at about two in the afternoon, under the guise of forgetting something she wanted to work on for the holiday weekend. All the General Dynamics buildings looked the same. They were two-story, gray, blue tempered glass structures with no see-through windows. The day was sunny and warm, about eight-five degrees, and much of the complex was cleared out because many people had left early or taken the day off entirely to make it a four-day weekend and head out to the desert for camping.

Nicole was wearing a gray wig and a little makeup to age her a bit, making her a dead ringer for Regina Smith, who Ops had word was a Consortium scientist interested in probability cloud physics. She wore a white lab coat, dull gray skirt that extended past the knee, and polite black heels. The heels made Nicole perhaps an inch taller than Regina, but she figured no one would notice, and they didn't. And in this area of GD, retina scans weren't required.

Fingerprints were, but Radar had equipped Nicole for that with some brilliant technology. He had a pair of gloves that via three-dimensional printing had Regina's fingerprints. Much like Radar's robotic 'skin,' they were undetectable from the real thing.

Regina Smith often frequented GD but was presently on vacation in Hawaii. That was unlikely to be known to the line staff, given she was an irregular visitor anyhow. She was a project manager, not one of the day-to-day staff. Besides Regina's resemblance to Nicole, that was a key reason they had picked her to impersonate.

Nicole approached the main lobby and said into her concealed mike, "Well, I'm in."

"Good job," said Medina as she sat in the passenger seat of a large Dodge Sprinter with an Amazon logo on the side, Sam behind the wheel. In '19, a huge Amazon delivery depot had been built on the hill next to GD, part of a steady rising of hills along Scripps Poway Parkway that led to the 67, which took drives to Ramona and the 78, and from here to Julian, where Sam had his fixer-upper. Trucks moved in an out constantly. One sitting by the side of the road was utterly inconspicuous, even to security-conscious GD. That's because drivers were constantly loading up and then pausing to check directions on their phones before they headed out like worker bees leaving the hive.

"I hope she's careful," said Sam.

Medina looked at him. "Forget that. I hope you can drive if we have to get moving."

"I can handle it," said Sam, looking worried. Then he switched frequencies and said, "You read me, Thunder?"

"Crickey, sorry, too loud." Pause. "That's better. Yeah, I'm fine."

He was parked to the northwest, about two blocks west, in the parking lot of a Carl's Jr. that was part of a larger mall area that included a credit union, gym, sandwich shop, and other small storefronts. It was across from a Hampton Inn, the normal staying place for those vendors visiting GD. The area was quiet. This was an industrial area, but most of the large employers, like GEICO insurance, had converted to at-home workers some time ago. Most of the general foot traffic was now purely from GD.

John Bogut, a.k.a. Thunder, was an elemental channeler with an affinity for electricity, hence the nickname. Now fifty-four, Thunder had a chiseled, weathered face with gray hair, blue eyes, and a pointed gray beard. He was a sturdy man, probably six feet two and in the 220 range.

Australia was his home base. He was born in Philadelphia, but when he was twelve, he got in a fight at school and channeled for the first time, though he didn't know it then. His mom had relatives in Australia, so the family moved to Brisbane, mostly because his parents wanted to keep him out of trouble until he matured and learned about channeling. He joined Ops back in 1986 when he was 19 and worked primarily Russia and Asia.

"Good," said Sam. "Ashley?"

"I'm in position," she said.

Now twenty-seven, Ashley McMillian had a fetching little bob cut. Her face was attractive and round, with light blue eyes, brownish and blonde hair, and a body that was purely round in the right places. She had large breasts pushing even her bulky shirt, and her pants were tight on her shapely bottom. Ashley had one of those bodies that made men drool. She was five-five and a sturdy 140 pounds.

A graduate of Portland State, Ashley had joined Ops right out of college. Her parents still lived in Centralia, Washington.

Thunder and Ashley had been captured in 2019 by the Consortium and spent months in prison on Mars. Thy were brought back to Earth to be sacrificed to Quotient, but Ops saved them,[4] and they were part of the sixteen-member channeling team that had defeated Quotient on New Year's Day. Since then, they had spent some of their time in the Portland area, helping with recovery efforts after Portland's population was wiped out by Quotient back in September.[5] They had spent several weeks in the spring in Europe helping Radar with his operations in Europe to combat the war in Ukraine and Putin's paranormal plans as well.[6]

Ashley was in the parking lot of Home Depot sitting in a red Ford F350, just another casual shopper. She wore a black and gray shirt knotted between the breasts with jeans and jogging shoes. Her blonde hair was held back by a black and red checkered hairband. She had a very country and western look.

"Good. I guess we wait on our fine doctor."

"Doctor, I'm Renee Stella. Could you come this way, please? We need your help," said a woman who approached Nicole as she entered and headed for the lobby to get her check-in papers.

"Certainly," said Nicole with a smile.

A raven-haired beauty with a huge chest, thirty-year-old Renee had dark eyes, a dark face, and hair swept to the right that was plain and straight. Her main feature was her bosom. She wore a blue sweater over a gray skirt with black hose and shoes, looking business

---

[4] See 3.1 "Escape" and 3.4 "The Island the World Forgot"
[5] See TM 3.10 "The House by the River"
[6] See the comic series "Special Operations – the War Years" starting with issue # 4

professional. Her security badge clipped to her breast marked her as A-1 clearance.

Nicole was relieved the woman had introduced herself — that told Nicole that the real Regina did not know Renee, which was very fortunate, because there wasn't shit in Ops files about Renee.

Quickly, Nicole used her channeling abilities to probe the woman's aura. Blockers. Nicole didn't show any sign of anything, but this put her on alert as she said, "Do you have the time?"

In the car, that alerted Medina and Sam. Medina quickly began scanning the name they had overheard.

Renee said, "Yes, it's 2:12. This way, please."

"Where are we going?"

"Lab eight. There's something the higher ups," and she pointed at the ceiling, "want you to review immediately."

"Certainly," said Nicole, using what the files told her was pretty much Regina's response to everything.

They walked down a tall corridor and came to a room that looked like an airport hangar — large and open, with machinery and gears. But they crossed this room to a stairwell and went to a second-floor office. They were now along the Scripps Poway Parkway side of the building, closer to Thunder at Jack-in-the-Box than Sam and Medina at Amazon.

In this room was a projection screen and ten, fold-up gray chairs in an otherwise empty room. The window shades were open, so it was sunny and hot. Inside was a tall man with thin black hair and a hassled look wearing a blue suit and with his mouth open. He had tiny eyes and a tiny nose. Next to him in a red blouse and black skirt was Maureen Hollander.

"Hi, doc, nice to see you again," said Maureen, moving forward to shake hands. "This is Scott Nedelman. Have you two ever met?"

Nicole *really* hoped Ops' files were right. "No, we haven't. Charmed, sir."

"Yup," said Scott. His handshake was quick, weak, and clammy. Nicole though he was like a guy on nicotine withdrawal.

"I'll be in the cafeteria," said Renee, clearly bored. She exited.

Nicole put her hands on her hips and said, "Well, this is a surprise. What's so important?"

"The spread of the particles. It's infinitely stronger than we thought," said Scott nervously.

Nicole was puzzled. She nodded at the screen. "Are we going to see pictures?"

Scott shook his head. "No. We just used this room as it's the only one unoccupied."

"Oh." She now was nervous. If this got into hard science, she was way out of her depth. She'd been lucky to escape with a "B" in biology at USC.

However, that quickly turned out not to be a problem, though in a very bad way.

Suddenly, the door opened, and the real Doctor Regina Smith was standing there, using her card key. With her was Maureen.

Nicole turned and smiled. "Well, this is embarrassing."

Maureen glared and said, "Okay, one of you is a fake."

Nicole smiled. "Now I'm insulted! I'm *much* prettier than you," and she pointed at Regina, "even in this ridiculous wig."

And with that, she channeled hard. Nicole had manifested in Anaheim, still slightly under the influence of the 2004 probability cloud created in Arizona. As a result, she was infused with improbability tachyonic influx, so she could alter probability with tachyons. In grave danger, she channeled wind laced with probability to blow Maureen and Regina down the corridor. They were like bugs caught in a hurricane and flew.

Quickly, she turned and kicked Scott in the balls. He had been completely taken aback by the channeling, and clearly he wasn't paranormal. He yelped and fell as if he had been shot.

Nicole raced down the hall and shouted into her com, "We're fucked! Doc Smith is here! I'm blown!"

"We're coming in," shouted Sam.

Before Nicole could respond, seven golf clubs flew down the corridor at her. She channeled and stopped five, but one hit her in the gut and as she gasped and fell forward, another hit her in the face.

Maureen grabbed Regina. "Come on."

They raced for the elevator. Staggered, Nicole raced after her. But she was a fraction of a second too late.

Slamming the elevator doors that closed in her face, she said, "Shit."

Then she found the stairs.

***

Sam and Medina started to move, but they stopped, because they spotted Renee racing across the parking lot towards the east exit, which was a walkway towards the Amazon lot.

"We're holding, we've got Renee headed our way," he said, calling to the others.

Thunder snapped, "I'll go after the sheila."

He raced out of the JIB.

Ashley shouted, "Do I go in?"

Medina said, "No, stay back. If Maureen runs, she may well run that way."

Inside, Nicole raced down the stairs, but as she hit the bottom level, an earth channel threw her off balance and the door opened right into her face. Staggered, she fell backwards into the flight of stairs. Suddenly, a robotic arm reached from inside a room and dragged her inside.

"Hey, leggo!" she shouted, losing one of her shoes.

The door slammed shut. A blinding light turned on, and Nicole threw her hands over her heads and cried out in pain. The light was so bright it hurt even with her eyes shut and her hands over her head. She was utterly helpless.

Then it went dark.

She opened her eyes and found herself in a completely white room.

"Whoa."

Maureen's' voice came over the loudspeaker. "I hope you like the latest in war games from GD. It'll be amusing to see how long you last. Good-bye, fraud."

Then the walls began to . . . melt.

Nicole stumbled backwards and felt terror she hadn't felt since . . . since . . . well, ever. It was a raw fear that made her want to vomit. In fact, she did.

Then she lifted her head and couldn't move.

Somehow, she was now naked and held in a tight, tangled black widow's spider web. And approaching form the corner was a black widow spider the size of a Volkswagen. It had eight eyes, hairy legs, and huge jaws.

She screamed and wet herself.

"Stop crying and let's move," shouted Maureen, grabbing Regina again, pulling her towards the exit. Maureen had no desire to stick around and see what happened with Nicole. She's set off emergency alarms, getting the few remaining employees out. But in paranormal terms, they were alone and had no backup. She knew Renee had already raced for Amazon, and following their pre-set emergency plans, Maureen had to take Regina the opposite way.

"I can't! I hurt my foot on the beach last week!" she whined.

Maureen slapped her. "Knock off the whining! This is an emergency!"

Scott suddenly appeared. "Let's go."

They suddenly felt their hairs raise on their skin. Maureen reacted instantly, diving out the second-floor window into bushes below.

Regina and Scott cried out in pain as electricity shot through them, knocking them cold. Thunder had arrived.

Nicole shut her eyes, then looked down. "I can't be this ugly naked. This can't be real. *It can't be real!*"

Her body told her it was. Her mind told her it was. But logically, spiders the size of Volkswagen's couldn't exit.

Fortunately for her, she didn't know about CRSPR and what Sam Grant and Meredith Patience had found years ago . . . if she had, she probably would have passed out and died.

"Not real. Not real! Bullshit fakes, like critical reviews," she told herself, closing her eyes. She tugged at the webs, but they stuck like needles in her skin. She was bleeding from at least two dozen wounds.

The spider inched closer. Nicole was sure it was smiling.

Smiling, Maureen raced across the parking lot and jumped into one of the company cars, a white Camry. The keys were in it, standard protocol for company cars in case of an emergency requiring the area to be cleared.

Thunder looked out the window and saw her taking off.

"Crickey! Fuck me dead. Hold tight."

He channeled and ruptured the earth. Maureen had to steer around it, and that directed her into a tree. She jumped out of the disabled car, cursed, turned, and used TK to fire rocks from a planter at him. That was just cover. She broke for safety, running to the far fence, which had a gate which led to the parking lot of the Costco-Price Club next door. The opening in the gate was only for deliveries, but Maureen had the key.

Thunder was out of range now. He raced down the stairs, unwilling to risk a jump from the second story because there was nothing but concrete below him.

He got to the bottom just as she raced across the parking lot towards the store.

"Damn. I'm rooted already. Maybe it *is* a young man's world."

"Outta the way, boy," snapped Renee as she shoved twenty-one-year-old Kurt Carmichael away from his gray and purple Amazon van parked just outside the building. Like many others, Kurt had loaded up and once he was outside the gate set up his phone with a delivery route.

Renee took off. But Sam and Medina drove down the access road at that moment.

Renee tried to sideswipe them, but Medina dodged, as she was now at the wheel. Quickly, she turned around to give chase.

"Move it!" shouted Sam.

"Hey, I'm trying! This thing drives like a bulldozer!"

Renee turned left, west, on Scripps Poway Parkway, which was a large road with three lanes in each direction and a divider. Medina was right behind her and technically ran a red light, though it was really close. Once she was behind Renee, she said to Sam, "Buckle up."

Sam was already buckled up, but he grabbed the handrail.

Medina focused all her channeling on the road ahead and ruptured it, simultaneously using wind to push the truck to the right, which would drive it off the road.

"I got the skank!" shouted Medina triumphantly.

Renee ran off the now ruptured road and onto the grassy shoulder, over a sidewalk, through some bushes and a fence and crashed in the parking lot of GEICO Insurance. GEICO had long been a presence in San Diego and had built their building twenty years ago, but at this point it was closed as all the workers did their business remotely.

Medina slowed and Sam jumped out to give chase. Renee had a good head start and was clearly running, not even looking back or attempting to channel. She wanted escape.

Sam ran, but his arthritis slowed him despite the adrenaline surge. Well, that and being in his fifties.

Medina paused, jumped out of the truck, and channeled water from the now completely broken sprinklers towards Renee in a wave. Like a battering ram, it headed right for her.

But Renee was quicker. She used TK to fling rocks from a landscaping planter near the door and it shattered, setting off alarms everywhere. She ducked inside.

Sam raced forward. He knew that because the police knew this was an active Ops investigation, they wouldn't respond unless Ops requested it.

Medina now raced to catch up, shouting, "Wait, Sam! You need me to cover you!"

"Cover me," said Thunder into the com to Ashley, who had started her car and was driving from Home Depot, which was on the west side of Costco, towards the entrance, which was the destination of Maureen, who was running form the east side of Costco and GD.

"You've got it," she shouted.

Maureen raced for the entrance. The road around the Costco was blocked at the front for foot traffic, so cars couldn't just circle around in front of the store, a change made a few years earlier. An attendant was pushing in carts. Maureen raced inside as if to make a customer service exchange, stepped into the line, then moved past. The two elderly people checking receipts on the way out didn't pay her any mind.

Thunder raced up on foot. Ashley approached from the opposite direction, driving up the west and much more narrow side as this parking lot was pinned between the Costco and Home Depot buildings. She had to stop by the food court because the road was blocked. She turned and found a parking spot and got out. This delay allowed Thunder to catch up with her.

"She went inside," snapped Thunder, pointing.

They raced for the entrance. A tall, older man moved to see their card and Thunder said, "Piss off, mate, we're here to rob the place."

Stunned, the man fell back. Ashley followed and smiled. "I'm with him."

Once inside, they were on the side with electronics. The entrance attendant called security.

"There!" shouted Ashley, seeing Maureen duck between rows of candy and nuts.

They moved instantly. Ashley and Thunder had worked together for years and spent months trapped on Mars in a Consortium prison in late 2019 and early 2020. They didn't need explanations or plans. Ashley went left, Thunder went right, and they had Maureen pinned.

She moved to channel, hurling the displays down, but while that got in Ashley's way, Thunder was able to dodge and tackle her. They landed hard, and her head snapped back and hit the concrete floor, like a quarterback taking a hard sack just as the pass was released.

"She's out colder than an Alaskan Christmas," said Ashley, checking her vitals. Maureen had a slight bleed on the back of her head.

"Yup."

"You two, freeze! You have a lot of explaining to do."

Ashley and Thunder looked at each other and laughed.

Screaming, Nicole shut her eyes and said, "I will not believe I can be eaten by a spider! *It can't happen!*"

She waited . . . and then opened her eyes when she realized she was still breathing.

The white walls had returned.

"God damn . . . it actually fucking worked. I've never been so happy to see an empty room in my life."

The empty rooms of the GEICO building were huge, because the building had primarily been a call center. All the furniture had been stripped. This was not what Renee had sought. She had run into a building that had absolutely no cover.

Racing for the far exit, she was far too late. Sam caught up to her and pulled his .32. "Hold it, tits!"

Renee turned to channel, but Medina was faster. She sent in earth from just outside the door. It was very wet, part of a planter that had been recently watered, and basically had the effect of a giant mudball. It slammed into her like a runaway truck, driving her hard into the far wall.

Medina and Sam raced forward. Renee struggled to get up enough to channel, but the problem was there was nothing in the office for her to hurl with TK.

Sam put the gun to her head. "I'm not playing."

That was enough. Renee put up her hands and said, "I want a lawyer."

Medina quickly shot her with a sedative and said, "Fuck that, lady. Ops is a military operation. Your lawyer can kiss my ass."

Sam laughed. "I never used to get away with saying things like that."

"Being a woman has privileges," said Medina with a smile. Sam rolled his eyes.

Thunder suddenly came over the com. "We've knocked Maureen cold."

"We've got the D-cup girl. Let's get our bitches on ice and check on the others, especially Nicole. She's still inside," said Nicole.

Nicole made her way out of the room much more easily than she had anticipated. She just pushed opened the door.

"How about that," she said, looking around the hallway in surprise.

Scott and Dr. Smith were gone. In fact, everyone was gone.

Nicole raced outside into the sun. Her com had been damaged. But everyone was long gone.

"Well, this is a fine welcome," she said, putting her hands on her hips and turning in a 180 looking for . . . anyone.

That's when the building imploded.

Chapter Four
Consortium Conspirators
Friday, July 2, 2021

"Well, you have to admit, they clean up after themselves," said Nicole as she and the rest of the Ops team stared at the pile of rubble that had been the General Dynamics scientific research building.

"It's not funny," snapped Sam. "They know something and now we're in the dark."

"Hey, gimme a break," snapped Nicole right back at him. "I went in there on my own and broke the case, and then got tossed in a room where I thought I was naked and about to be eaten by a giant spider. I can make jokes if I want!"

Sam was taken aback. "Sorry."

"It's okay. I'm sorry, too. I'm just . . . I deal with it by denial."

"Fair enough."

"Besides, I still haven't quite settled down from being tied up naked and nearly eaten by the giant black widow spider."

"*You what*?" asked Sam, and he looked instantly panicked.

Nicole stepped back. "I, uh, I think it was a dream or something. I was tied up naked fighting a giant spider, a fucking black widow."

Sam looked at Medina and said, "Secure this whole place."

"The rubble? Why? What's wrong?"

Sam snapped, "CRISPR technology. Meredith and I had a run in with a giant spider a while back — also a black widow.[7] There could be anything crawling around this place, including aliens."

Medina saw the look in Sam's eye and said, "I'm on it."

As she stepped back to use the phone with more privacy, Nicole asked, "Uh, since I caused this shit-storm, what is crispier? A type of KFC recipe?"

Sam shook his head, ignoring her joke. "CRISPR is a way to rewrite DNA. In the '80s, scientists at Osaka University in Japan noticed unusual and repeated DNA sequences next to a gene they were studying in a common bacteria. The sequences were part of a sophisticated immune system that bacteria use to fight viruses. The Consortium got hold of the technology, and researchers had discovered that the bacterial system could be harnessed to make precise changes to the DNA of humans, as well as other animals and plants. I've seen one piece of the Consortium's CRISPR handiwork, a giant spider. We think it might also be how Kosar cloned those Subject Seven aliens we ran across in Wyoming in '17."[8]

Thunder, Ashley, and Nicole looked at each other with surprise and a little skepticism. They weren't familiar with any of these events.

Sam snapped, "They may have drugged you to make you more susceptible, but it wouldn't surprise me if the spider was real." He frowned. "In fact, that's likely, if they were there to stop paranormals. Giant spiders don't do well against paranormals, not if there's just one. Probably a drug to disorient you."

"It felt real."

"All hallucinations do," said Thunder quickly. "But Sam's right. If there's a risk they were using something nasty, best to shut it down right proper."

Sam suddenly rubbed his chin. "Only thing is, CRISPR was driven by Kosar, who is long dead. Obviously, it's not him, so who's driving the research for the Consortium now?"

---

[7] In TM 2.13 "The Second Death of Abagail Starr"
[8] In TM 2.6 "Naked and Afraid"

***

"Interesting," said Connor McLaughlin to himself as he studied a vial through dirty protective glasses as it neared midnight in Europe.

His Consortium lab was in Glickstenstein, a tiny country of only one hundred square miles wedged between Poland and Belarus run by a TM named Valeria von Strussman, one of the six TMs that had launched the Golden Age project in Tiera del Fuego. She ruled by lineage. The country wasn't part of NATO, nor was it Russian friendly. It just existed.

They didn't need friends. They had *plenty* of firepower to defend themselves, and everyone knew it.

Valeria owned a castle, which had been converted into a prison primarily for political prisoners. But in the bunker levels beneath the castle were experimental labs and living quarters for Valeria and her guests. They were lavish room and expensive labs. Valeria didn't care. She was worth several billion dollars.

At 34, Valeria spoke with an accent that sounded Polish, as many in Glickstenstein, including her, spoke that as a native language. She was also beautiful. She prided herself on her beauty. Her chin was a little too angular, but otherwise she was poster-perfect. Her eyes were sky-blue. Her hair was dark, long, and straight, and framed her face perfectly. Her bosom was larger than normal and rode high, her hips the perfect ratio, and her appearance impeccable. She did this without a glamour, which a TM could use to alter his or her appearance to look younger or older — the aura could affect DNA. To Valeria, a glamour was a mark of failure. Today she wore a black sweater over gray pants with black boots.

"We must talk," snapped Valeria as she entered what looked to be a chemistry lab with several tables, several active vials of chemicals, and a working Bunsen burner. On a stool in front of the table with the Bunsen Burner was Connor.

"Of course," he said, removing the glasses. "Give me a moment to end the experiment."

Valeria nodded curtly and studied her latest Consortium project leader. She'd been through a couple. But she liked Connor the most. Now 18, Connor looked like his father, Dave, just a younger version. But he had the hard inner core and steel eyes of his late mother, Andrea Voodoo.[9] Like his father, Connor had fair, blond hair swept to the right, glasses, and a handsome face with sharp blue eyes. But his face was rounder, and his frame lankier like his mother's ostrich-sized shape. He wore a loose-fitting mint green dress shirt that wasn't tucked in, jeans, and red and white sneakers.

Once he finished, he turned to her and said, "I can see you're upset. How can I help?"

Valeria didn't stand on ceremony. She quickly said, "Our efforts to end Ops' research by removing Dr. Tang from the board may have failed. They tracked Hollander and have taken her and Renee captive."

Connor frowned. "This is serious. We need to link in Judge Rod."

"Agreed."

Connor reached with his left hand for his laptop and used it to cue up a visual meeting with Judge Rod via a Consortium secure app and link.

Now 74, Judge Rodchester Norton was known as Judge Rod, or simply asshole. He'd been one of the most hard-nosed judges until his retirement in 2012. He presided over some of the most critical trials in Chicago history. He'd gone from small-town Iowa boy to one of the most prestigious jobs in Chicago. On his retirement, he found he enjoyed the Bahamas and spent most of his time there looking for fine young men, as Rod was gay. But he still owned a home in Evanston, outside Chicago.

He was also a major player in the Society of Jack-O'-Lanterns, the Society for short, an old organization that was run by the rich to help the downtrodden. Well, they helped by using slavery to lead to freedom, usually taking sexually abused women, enslaving them for a

---

[9] Andrea's long history opposing Ops and working with the Sixteen ended when she died in June Bauer's body in TM 2.6 "Naked and Afraid"

period, then letting them walk rich or stay. Most stayed. Most of the Society was really there for the sexual benefits of the rich members, and largely their plans worked, so they kept rolling. The Consortium heavily infiltrated it, however, and used it to find women likely to generate paranormal abilities. Many had been killed in their experiments.

The Consortium was heavily represented on the thirteen member inner council, which included Judge Rod. He was one of the thirteen members of the inner council. And with Dave McLaughlin having lapsed into the basement and self-pity as he tried to rescue his late wife from Hell, where she'd been and escaped only to be sent back, Judge Rod had taken over mentorship of Connor and the Golden Age plan. What the hell, he had time.

Appearing on the screen in a green and white Hawaiian shirt, he clearly was on the beach somewhere beautiful. At six-one and 205 pounds, he was still in excellent condition, though his skin was very wrinkled.

"Well, this is an interesting call." He was sitting in the living room of his condo, apparently using the phone behind the bar, because all they could see was him in a red and white Hawaiian shirt and bottles of liquor on shelves behind him.

"Sorry to bother you, but we have a situation," said Connor.

Rod kept mixing a drink. "No problem, m'boy. Is it just us."

"I am here," said Valeria haughtily.

"Ah, fine. What's the problem?"

"Ops has Hollander and Renee."

Rod nodded. "Interesting. Well, we knew this could happen."

"They will talk," said Valeria, as if spitting out the name of a disease.

"It doesn't matter," said Rod. "There's enough of a paper trail where someone at Ops will figure out the route leads back to Tonya eventually even *without* Hollander and Renee. But they have no real reason to suspect her of anything. She's always been purely a paper manager, especially since that fallout with Cly Hamilton a while back."[10]

"Surely Ops will talk to her?" said Valeria.

"Like I said, we knew this could happen. It was worth the risk to silence Tang. No one can pick up her end of the research and figure it out in time to stop the Golden Age. I don't know they'll even talk to Tonya."

"How do we contact her?" asked Connor. "We have to at least let her know the situation."

"I'm sure she knows anyhow, but she's in Madrid, right? Just send her a coded cable. Has she gotten anywhere with finding Jabbar?"

"No," said Valeria grimly.

Laura Jabbar had been the Society's lead torturer for several years. But they found out last year she had been covertly working with a group on the inside to bring down the Society from within. She'd been a key aid to the late Calypso, a former assassin who played a large role in the rebellion. Many of the Society double-agents had been found and dealt with, and other didn't know enough to be concerning. But everyone was concerned about Jabbar, who had disappeared.[11]

Rod nodded. "Well, nothing we can do about that now. Tonya is going to be visited by Ops, so she better get ready."

"She has a captive now, Helena Gibbronowski, that might lead to Jabbar."

"Anyhow, what's important is the Golden Age. We need to make sure nothing with Tonya leads back to Connor, just in case Ops does dig up Tonya and she actually caves in."

"We are secure," said Valeria confidently. "Shouldn't we aid her in her defense?"

"No. We can't draw attention to ourselves." He chuckled. "Besides, they're too late. Even if we rolled over like Trump's accountants and told them everything, they can't actually *do* anything about it."

---

[10] Tonya and Cly first appeared in the Society novel "Outside the Box"
[11] As was her intent, as shown in TM 4.1 "The Killer Inside"

"Very well," said Valeria. Judge Rod was one of the few people Valeria respected. He was very smart and very practical.

"Good. Remember, Tonya pretty much hangs in Madrid with Fred and Jill. They'll take care of her."

"Let us hope that is true," said Valeria.

Connor grimaced. He wasn't so sure, but he was the junior member. He'd taken up the mantle of the Golden Age operation, aided by Rod of course, when his father had more or less dropped out of the Society's plans. Dave had been shattered by their defeats and just wanted his wife back. Connor wanted a better world. And he knew the best way to achieve that was the Consortium. People weren't going to volunteer to do what was right. That's the reason they needed to be told what to do.

"I can't tell you what to do, but I think we're close," said Medina as she, Nicole, and Ashley ate in the Carl Junior's near the battle scene earlier in the day. It was about five in the evening now. Sam, Thunder, and Radar were still on site at the rubble of the General Dynamics building checking some things out.

"I can stay for the weekend, but I can't risk my acting," said Nicole to Medina. "I mean, sure, if we find Sunset and Morgana, I'll drop everything. But all I accomplished today was to get caught and nearly eaten by a spider."

"You're bloody wrong about that," said Thunder as he and Sam entered. Thunder chuckled.

"Hey, on this side of the Earth, I'm always right. Do I go to Australia and tell you you're wrong?" said Nicole with a smile.

"Crickey, I hope not. I got enough with her tellin' me I'm a dill without you adding on," he said, thumbing at Ashley.

Sam pulled over a chair, as the table had only four, and said, "You were hit by some type of hallucinogenic weapon. The spider was there, but even in your disoriented state you fought it off. The rest, like the nudity, was all in your head."

"Well, I figured that, because clothes don't just vanish, even in Ops!"

Nodding, Sam said, "True. Anyhow, that's all it was."

Nicole wiped her hands on a napkin and stood up. "Well, I'm heading up to Hollywood to check on my condo. Medina, call me if anything urgent comes up."

"You want company? I haven't been to Hollywood in a few months, and last time I was there, I was fighting to save the world, so I didn't see many famous people," said Ashley.

Nicole quickly shook her head and smiled politely but not warmly. "Sorry, I'll only be checking out my place quickly, then I have plans with friends. Maybe next time. Bye, all."

She left. Ashley looked at Medina and said, "Boy, she blew me off, didn't she?"

"She has problems right now. Don't take it personally," said Medina.

"Of course."

Sam snorted. "We are all gonna have problems soon. I contacted Shank and he's working with Miramar," said Sam, referring to General Lester Shank, head of the WSA, a global version of the NSA. "We've got transport out of here for us and our two "guests" in an hour. Let's get over to Miramar, get back to Vegas, and see what we can get out of them. We're running out of time and leads."

Chapter Five
The McGrath Group
Saturday, July 3, 2021

"We've learned nothing," said Sam the next morning with a frown as he, Medina, Thunder, Ashley, and one of Radar's robot bodies sat around the baseball diamond Sam had installed at the Vegas complex back when he was running things. The field was small but cute, like something a small semi-pro team would have with a chain-link fence and bleachers on the first and third-base sides. They were sitting on the third base side. They were warm. Even though it was only ten in the morning, it was already nine-two degrees. The sun was behind them. "Shank's interrogations failed. He's going to try drugs, but that could take hours if not days to get reliable information."

Sam wore a black and yellow checkered shirt with the sleeves rolled up and white sneakers. Radar wore a gray T-shirt with a print of Dolly Parton's boobs and black sneakers. Medina wore a pink blouse, black pants, and white heels. She was swatting at flies and yellowjackets attracted by her perfume. Thunder wore a dark green T-shirt with gray pants and brown shoes. Ashley wore a red bikini top with white shorts and sandals made from seashells.

Radar chuckled. "Don't worry. I did a lot of digging last night and we don't need Maureen and Renee anymore to tell us behind this. Just their presence here enabled me to break into some things related to General Dynamics, and I worked the trail back. I also got some help from Ortmayer, who took over the NSA last month."

"I knew Ortmayer when he was a gopher," said Sam with a laugh. "But he's a sharp guy."

"Yeah. Anyhow, I know who's managing this thing on the Consortium side. It's a woman named Tonya Duncan. And I know *exactly* where Tonya Duncan is. She's sitting on her ass in Madrid running Intertwine."

"What's an Intertwine? Some type of internet company?" asked Ashley.

"Nah. Insurance."

Sam snapped his fingers. "Sure, Intertwine. In terms of assets, they became the largest in the world last year, passed Allianz."

Everyone looked at him.

"What? Look, running field ops, I spent half my time dealing with insurance on everything from an exploding Ford Pinto to entire cities. You get interested in the stuff."

"Uh, yeah," said Medina.

"Anyhow, back to my point. Allianz is headquartered in Munich, just up the road from where I'm running Bundt's old division of Meridian Insurance," said Radar. "Let's go back a bit. Tonya ran and heavily owned Meridian. It was one of the assets that Intertwine purchased in '15 to pass up Allianz. Tonya moved up quick. She runs the whole fuckin' show now."

Thunder punched a fist into his hand. "Let's give this bloody sheila a sickie."

"Easy, Thunder. This ain't some comic book super-villain. Tonya's hooked into the Society and the Consortium at the *highest* levels. I have no idea what she can do. And she's keep a low profile, but she's been with Meridian and them for nearly thirty years. She started there right out of high school in the mid-90s. She's gotta have more power than the average gray-haired insurance executive. And from my surveillance, she's got a team."

"Surveillance?" asked Ashley.

"Hey, she's always been in my, uh, radar since I came back in '20. She had too much power and too much money and there were too many empty entries in the ledgers, so to speak. She funneled a ton of money to Kelkirk, but she did it well, and Intertwine is at the forefront of insurance for space travel. Anyhow, remember how I said she started at Meridian right at the beginning? Well, when she worked at Meridian in San Diego, one of her co-workers and fellow supervisors was . . . wait for it . . . wanna guess?"

"Your mother?" offered Sam.

"Cara Goodrich."

"*Of the Quartet*? Fuck me," said Sam.

"Blimey," added Thunder.

"But Tonya was never someone directly involved in *anything* that I could find, at least until now." He shook his head. "But no way it can be coincidence. Maybe she's not into the global warming part of the Consortium, but she's dirty as this fucking baseball infield."

"What's changed?" asked Sam.

"Mid-life crisis, I bet. Gray hair will do that to anyone," said Ashley, elbowing Thunder and laughing.

Ignoring her, Thunder asked, "Crickey, how did you tie this to her?"

"First, Ashley, I don't know what's changed now, unless we've drained the Consortium of paranormal assets enough to force her take charge. If she's TM and is immortal, obviously she's vested in keeping the world safe. Maybe she's been fighting by proxy. I don't know. I'd like to, but I don't. Second, I got wind of some unusual transactions a few weeks ago, which tied to Morrison's movements. Then last night I hacked into this using some encryption Shank's people picked up investigating GD in San Diego." He shared his screen to show an insurance policy. "This is a contract between the government of Glickstenstein and Tierra del Fuego guaranteeing six billion dollars in damage should events on June 21 result in catastrophic damage to the country."

"Is that legal?" asked Sam incredulously.

"It is because they're both Consortium laced countries. This is basically a deal between the governments of each country, which allowed Morrison's group to run their tachyonic spell on Tiera del Fuego's land and give them some security." Radar laughed. "In fact, they paid out like three million in damages thanks to the plane crash and all the damage at the airport."

"I wish we had wrecked more," said Medina sarcastically.

"Uh, okay. So, Tonya is in Madrid. Spain," said Ashley.

"Yeah, it's still there, McMillian. Aliens haven't moved it," said Radar dryly. "Anyhow, Osa is presently in Europe with one of my robot bodies looking into some other stuff, so I can use her. And myself. Uh, you know what I mean."

"I get the feeling you don't think it's that easy," said Sam.

"Uh, well, maybe. For the moment, let's just assume we can find Tonya. She has two major league bodyguards, Pastor Fred and his daughter, Jill."

"Major League as in that bad 80s movie or a major threat?" asked Ashley with a smile.

"As in they can kill any of us one on one fifty times over before we piss ourselves. So going in requires a bit of a plan. It's not something you do on a whim. But I've got help over there. It's time to call Little Jack and get the McGrath Group in on the plan."

"The McGrath Group is thrilled to help," said Little Jack McGrath with a broad, shit eating grin on his face as he rose and spread his arms so Radar and Medina could fully see him on the screen in Vegas. He was in Europe, so it was late evening and he was in an office somewhere.

"You realize we're not paying you," said Medina, laughing before she even finished the sentence.

Little Jack put on a mock wounded face and hit his chest. "You wound me, Miss Kane, wound me, I say!"

"Aw, get off it."

Little Jack laughed. He was a charismatic young man who enhanced that with exceptional politeness and people skills. He got things done, but not in a dictatorial fashion. No, he did it the *right* way.

Now thirty-one, he had just a hint of a wrinkle around his eyes, but otherwise looked abnormally young. At six feet and two inches tall, he had presence but wasn't overtly big. He sported short blond hair and usually a huge grin. Despite very big ears, he was attractive. His green eyes made him look like a cat.

He dressed casually and in a very standardized fashion. In public, he almost always wore the same outfit: old jeans, white tennis shoes, a black dress shirt with white vertical stripes, no tie, and always the top button unfastened. He wore the same outfit the way Superman wore the same crime-fighting costume.

Little Jack and his late sister, Sherry, grew up together. They were born to Big Jack McGrath and his first wife, Danielle. Little Jack came in 1990, Sherry in 1991. Big Jack McGrath was a legend in both business and the TM business, but a serious back injury in '85 forced him to retire to the purely fiscal end of the TM business. A wizard with real estate and mining, he was worth several billion dollars. Danielle was his acolyte before she became his wife, and she died in a battle with the Head in late 1991, just months after giving birth to Sherry.

Lisa was his half-sister, and they didn't meet until she was fifteen, but he always accepted her as a full sister, showing the hospitality and family loyalty his father had engrained in him. Little Jack learned everything about TM and business from his father. He idolized him, and when his father died in 2012 from brain cancer, Little Jack came to realize it was up to him to carry on the family name.

As for Lisa and Sherry, well, they were incestuous, but everyone had flaws. The one drawback to being incredibly rich, incredibly invested in torture magic, and incredibly powerful was isolation. They had no peers and had turned to each other in a very intimate manner.

But Little Jack's obsession for the perfect deal and his interest in TM led him to conspire with the late Gary Hart, founder of the International News Network (INN), Dr. Robert Kosar, and serial killer TM Marc Bundy to attempt to open a portal to restore the first torture magicians, Elkrod and Quafara, to Earth and under their control.

The result was catastrophic. All six conspirators died when Ops broke up the attempt to open the portal. Little Jack was infused with a dramatic mix of tachyons, portal energy, and psychic heat. Driven insane, he instinctively portaled and was found wandering aimlessly in Detroit a few days later by Ops.[12]

Sylvester Starnes, the Immortal Man and head of Special Operations, drew the power out of Little Jack, restoring him to normalcy. But Little Jack's time had dramatically changed him. He had seen all times and dimensions simultaneously, but jumbled, like plays in a football game in the wrong order. But what was clear was his destiny if he did *not* change his ways. Moreover, he was the one hope of redemption for his siters, who were in Hell. He had to change to save them, save himself, and save millions — and he did. His sincerity was confirmed by a mental scan by telepath Mary Richardson. Then he took over Ops in early 2018.

But when he proposed to Joy Delaney-McGrath earlier in the year after some of the Ops team went to and returned from Hell, he retired. He started the McGrath Group, because somehow the shift in tachyonic makeup of our dimension when the portal to Hell opened put all his scrambled memories into one cohesive unit. He knew this was what he had to do to safeguard the world from the threats to come. Presently, they were working out of an ancient underground bunker built during World War II on the outskirts of Florence, Italy.

"Well, I guess we can do a job for free to help out old friends," said Little Jack, pretending to think it over.

"How generous. Radar, fill him in," said Medina.

"Thanks, big-ears, 'cause this one's vital. We got a hit on a major Consortium player that's suddenly taken center stage. She's gonna be well-guarded, and I wanna move fast. Since you and your posse are in Europe already, I figured you could help us out quickly, 'cause our target is in Spain."

---

[12] As outlined in TM series two

"Sure. I'm kind of in the middle of a mess, but Joy and my sisters will be glad to help. I've rung them."

"Good," said Radar. "I've got my gold robotic self in Germany, then there's another humanoid robot in France keeping an eye on Chase." Chase was recovering from her 2020 kidnapping ordeal and recovering from Stockholm syndrome in France. "I can spare him for this. I've got a second humanoid robot that's on European detail and he's in Warsaw with Osa. So that gives us three of me, Osa, and your three, that's six. I think we can handle it with that group."

"Dude, I'd think three of you could handle it by yourself," said Little Jack.

"I'm worried they might have robotic defenses, and we have multiple potential strike points."

"Good point. Well, this is a good chance to get the girls some field work. They're still . . . still getting used to being alive."

"You'll die here," said Sherry, waving the knife in front of the victim.

"Everyone talks, Jaworski," said Lisa menacingly, pointing at him.

Twenty-nine, Lisa was a thin but well-built, sexy brunette with long, chestnut brown hair that extended halfway down her back. It was straight. She had a round face, supple lips, green eyes, and freckles. Clearly, she worked out to stay in shape and liked to be tan. Lisa wore a pink blouse over navy green leggings with black booties. Her skin glistened with suntan lotion.

Thirty, Sherry was a bit more buxom, also with chestnut brown hair, but hers was wavy and framed a more sexual face. She did not have freckles, but she also had green eyes. She wore a white blouse with black swirls, a red mini-skirt, and red heels.

After their death in January of 2018, the two sisters had been in Hell. Besides being incestuous from virtually the minute they met in 2007, the women had committed innumerable grievous acts on innocents, though rarely directly. But Little Jack's actions redeemed them, as did their own decisions in Hell, and they were resurrected in early 2021 in the bodies of two women who looked almost identical to them who had died in a car accident outside of Vegas on I-11. They found Little Jack and reunited the family. They were now part of the McGrath Group.

Lisa picked up a pair of pliers and said, "Let's start with teeth. As fat as you are, not being able to eat is our best torture."

Sherry suddenly put her hand out. "Wait. Wait, we can't torture him."

Lisa looked at her half-sister with surprise. "Why not? We need information."

"No, no, remember, we're here from Hell because we were redeemed. We have to change our ways. Torture is evil."

Frowning, Lisa put down the pilers on the table and put her hand son her hips. "I don't know about that. Every government in the world uses torture."

"Americans don't," said Jaworski quickly and purely out of self-interest.

Sherry looked at him with disgust. "Grow up. Ever hear of Guantanamo Bay? Oh, and waterboarding is torture, no matter what any ridiculous court of law says."

"Forget him. This is an important point. I mean, how are we supposed to be good people if we don't know the ground rules?" asked Lisa worriedly.

Sherry frowned. "This is a valid point. I mean, I think that's what life is about, making choices, but how can you choose if you don't know what's right?" She shook her head. "We should ask my brother."

"Or Joy. She's just across the hall in the kitchen," said Lisa, pointing.

"Okay, let's roll."

They walked across the hallway, securing the door with aural and physical locks, and after crossing the stone corridor with medieval walls worthy of any horror show castle, they were in a large and surprisingly modern kitchen. Standing before a stainless-steel refrigerator and staring hopelessly into it was Joy Delaney-McGrath.

Now twenty-eight-years-old, the newlywed was very pretty, though not gorgeous. She had a nice round bottom, perky breasts, good legs, and a happy face. Her hair tended to be straight and parted in the middle, and although a natural blonde she often dyed it lighter. Her eyes were a dull blue, her face pretty, though her nose was a little big. Joy was the type of girl that looked good in nice clothes and make-up, looked average without them, and basically was pretty enough that she could get by if she was willing to play to her assets.

When she'd manifested her channeling in November 2017, she had been having an affair with her boss. At the time, Joy was a typical twenty-something woman in Chicago — she just wanted to get along at her job, spend weekends hanging with her friend Leah, and take care of her mom, who had early onset Alzheimer's. Yeah, Joy's life was perfect. She wasn't having the affair to get a better position at the company or get a new husband. She just liked having fun and liked shopping for clothes. And subconsciously, she was strongly drawn to men in power, because she wasn't a decision-maker.

That made her unusual channeling ability all the more unlikely to manifest, but it did. She was not a pure elemental channeler. Her abilities were more akin to channeling a basic force, that being electricity, for her channeling had an influence on the brain on the person with which she had eye contact. They had to do as she instructed.

But she wasn't comfortable using her ability. For one thing, she needed eye contact, which wasn't always easy in a battle. And after a briefly experiment of controlling others, she got a little overconfident and wound up captured in 2018 while the team looked for the Smile. Chase and others freed her, but that experience made her realize how difficult her ability could be. It wasn't reliable.[13]

But just weeks after that, she first met Little Jack.

Then everything changed.

And then he proposed, and everything changed again.

---

[13] See TM 2.14 "Cycle of Abuse" and issues # 1-5 of the comic book "Special Operations – The Untold Tales"

When Lisa and Cherie had returned from Hell, Joy wasn't sure what to make of it all. She'd been excited about leaving Ops for the McGrath Group and avoiding combat, trying to help people in non-violent ways. She wasn't sure how two women from Hell fit that model, and more importantly, she was also worried they would be a bad influence on Little Jack. But so far, everything had worked out.

Little Jack had explained that the women, like he had been, were changed. They were reincarnated. Their old actions were not them, any more than his were until he was split across dimensions. Joy believed that, though not all did. She never asked about anything the sisters had done before, though she knew, as did everyone, that they had been incestuous.

Joy looked at them, seeing the confusion on their faces. Lisa leaned against the wall and folded her arms over her chest while Sherry said, "Joy, we need a ruling."

"Ruling?" asked Joy, slowly shutting the refrigerator door. This wasn't the first time they had asked. She didn't like making decisions, but most of their questions were extremely cut and dried.

"Yes. We caught Jaworski and are trying to get the information my brother needs," said Sherry.

Joy's eyes lit up. "That's a good deal! That guy is high on the want list!"

"But he won't talk," said Sherry, almost in a pout. "Now, Lisa was going to torture him, but I think that's wrong and worry that will send us back on the road to Hell."

"Every government uses torture," said Lisa, clearly pinning her beliefs on this single, though valid, point.

Joy bit her lip, then leaned against the refrigerator and said, "This is kind of a gray area. I don't know if I'm qualified to decide this one."

"Well, I am."

They turned to see Little Jack strolling through the door, patting Lisa on her left shoulder as he entered. He smiled broadly and added, "The answer is that the answer is maybe, but for Jaworski, it doesn't matter. We can deal with him later. Right now, we've got an important job for Ops and are taking a little trip."

"We are?" asked Sherry, arching an eyebrow.

Little Jack nodded and smiled broadly. "We are, sis. Pack the bags, 'cause we're goin' to Spain."

Chapter Six
Spain
Sunday, July 4, 2021

"Lack of planning is what brings down most of these endeavors," said fifty-one-year-old Tonya Duncan. She was a sultry woman with wrinkles but still an attractive face, pink lipstick and blush framing good bones. Her hair was now gray, saving her the need to dye it blonde or white as she had most of her life. Her hair was cut short. Her figure was still superb. She had a little weight in the legs and behind, but she was only twenty pounds over her weight from twenty years earlier. She loved to work out on the treadmill three times a week.

Unlike most TMs who used glamours, a way of manipulating the body's genetics via the aura to appear younger or more attractive, Tonya, like Valeria, took pride in herself and displayed who she was. She wasn't willing to waste power on an aura, because frankly she thought she looked like hot shit, which she did for her age.

"That's quite true," said Fred, smiling as he poured her a cup of coffee. Fifty-six-year-old Fred Lippert was a defrocked priest of the Catholic Church. He was tall at six-three with broad shoulders and an awkward gait. He had a broad smile and a couple growths on his face, a gray mustache and wavy gray hair, but oddly cold eyes. He put on the air of a friendly pastor, but something underneath his demeanor seemed more aggressive.

A man with a dark past, he sat at the round kitchen table to Tonya's right. In Madrid, it was eight in the morning. And it was already warm, nearly eighty degrees. Tonya had just risen and wore black workout shorts and a white sports bra. Her figure, despite her age, could bear the exposure. Fred wore a puffy black pirate shirt with jeans.

They were in the living room of Tonya's glorious, isolated hacienda that sat on eighty acres in a secure compound just outside Madrid. The structure had one main building of two stories, a recessed building with three stories, and a bell tower behind that. There was a lower level that ran along the front of the driveway and was a single story. The kitchen was in the bottom of the main building, so they were overlooking the lush grass that composed the front yard. Trees and grass were all around the building. There were few flowers or other vegetation, but it was well maintained.

"I learned long ago . . . I don't like fighting. I like directing. I've always kept in the shadows . . . but this is our last chance to save the world . . . I can't sit on my ass any longer. When Cly came up with her thing, I sort of dropped out. I just didn't see that thing working out. But . . . I can't take a backseat any longer. The Quartet, Calico, they sought to move humanity away from doomed Earth. Cly thinks her thing means global warming doesn't matter, but she's gone a little nuts. It *does* still matter. Who wants a world of boiling water and no animals? The Golden Age plan is by far the only sensible plan left in the cookbook. We will instantly stop any further greenhouse gases. There's a chance to save us by doing this. We haven't quite passed the point of no return, though some in the Consortium think that."

"I don't," said Fred.

She smiled. "I know . . . anyhow . . . Cara is . . . is gone." She winced, still pained by the death of one of her best friends. "I've got to step up and be part of saving us. I've no desire to be immortal on a world that looks like the leftover set of a *Mad Max* film. Sure, some people are going to die. It's like less than two percent. That's nothing."

Fred nodded. He knew the math. Those were low figures, and even those came out to well over 150,000 people. But he figured most of them were the weak and frail and soon to die anyhow, so he was on board. No, ethics weren't his concern. Battle was his concern, which he voiced by stating. "You know Ops can likely find us now."

She shrugged. "Of course. I'm sure they've always known where we are. Radar is resourceful, and I'm too prominent a figure to hide. But I've never threatened them before. I don't think they'll bother me now."

"I think they will."

She looked at him. "You know all I have been through in my life. Do you think they scare me?"

"No," he said immediately.

She smiled. "Besides, I have you and Jill."

He rose. "We'll stay alert. What are your plans today?"

"Head to the aquatic park to continue my, ah, talk with Helena Gibbronowski."

"Ah," he said.

"You and Jill remain here. I have security at the park, and I can disguise my aura and set a trap here. Do not leave for any reason. I'm expecting another security aide to arrive as well. Here are the details," said Tonya, sending a text.

"We'll be on the grounds, and regular security still has the perimeter. We'll be ready for anything," said Fred.

Smiling, she kissed his cheek. "I know I can count on you. Be safe."

"Of course. You as well."

She left the room. Fred checked his phone. No messages, other than Tonya's text. He then turned to exit when his daughter, Jill, entered.

Perky Jill had short, straight blonde hair that was straight with bangs in front, a pert nose, blue eyes, and a round, pleasing face. She was one of those people that always looked perky and always had perfect hair — she used to joke she had better hair than Sarah Michelle Gellar in *Buffy*. She was wearing a white turtleneck, jeans, black boots, and a smile.

"Hi," she said, kissing her father on the cheek. "Where's Tonya?"

"About to head out for the park."

Jill nodded. She was twenty-six and in good physical condition, someone that didn't work out much but did eat well. "Okay. You want me to watch the front gate?"

"Yes. You know how she gets when she works. Help her on her way, then report back here."

Jill nodded. "I'll be ready. Just let me know what I can do to help."

"Spain is a weird place," Joy said to Osa as they drove towards the hacienda where Tonya was staying. Joy wore a pink blouse and a white skirt with red shoes and white hose. She looked like a classy businesswoman. Osa wore black running pants with white stripes and a dark red top, her long black hair pulled back in a ponytail. Her top was sleeveless, showing off tan and fit muscles. They were dressed to fit their intent to blend in with the community.

"In some ways, though admittedly, I've only been here a few times, mostly to cover events for INN," said Osa, and she didn't elaborate, lost in thought.

Currently thirty-three-years-old, former INN reporter Osa Carerra a long but attractive face with interestingly contrasted oval eyes that were dark brown. Her skin was a Mediterranean dark mix. By shaving her eyebrows and painting them, she had an unusually intense appearance. She was wearing make-up, primarily to make her supple lips look moist. Her long hair was so black it looked blue in the sunlight during the daylight hours, but the waves and folds from her ears to her shoulders had just a touch of silver highlights.

Carrera was more than a pretty face, for she had extensive tendrils in the paranormal. Originally, she had been part of the Society due to her parents being upper echelon members. After spending some time in the inner circle at the Society, she joined INN as a correspondent, spending three years in the Hollywood office watching the late Gary Hart's activities. Just before Christmas in 2017, she stumbled on the plans of Kelkirk and Sigurdsson to, in varying degrees, kill millions to save the earth from global warming. Teaming up with others, she worked to overthrow the Society from within, but about a month ago had come to Ops for sanctuary, concerned the Society had discovered her double-role.

Carrera was an elemental channeler, not a user of TM like many in the Society and the Consortium. She'd survived in the Society by withstanding a brutal torture and refusing to fold two years earlier. For seventeen days, she was bound to a chair daily and given random, periodic electrical shocks throughout my body. Most people tortured in this fashion confessed within days or were driven insane. Carrera was the only person that never confessed and never snapped.

After the collapse of the Kelkirks a few months earlier, Osa had come to Ops for protection. Other than one quick field op with the late Colin Ridgeway,[14] she'd basically been confined to the property for her own safety. Her parents lived in New Mexico and were under Ops' guardianship as well. But in May, after helping Searly stop Michelle Guzman in Anaheim as part of finding Society member Rae Jorgensen dead,[15] Radar had asked him to help her with a couple assignments in Europe, which she had undertaken, as she as going stir-crazy hanging out in Vegas.

"Osa? You okay?" asked Joy.

Nodding, Osa said, "Yes, just . . . thinking. I'm nervous, Joy. I'm not . . . I've been on the run a long time. It's different doing the stalking instead of being the stalked."

"You'll be fine," said Joy, but she was nervous as well. She'd never been a huge field ops fan. She liked helping, but mostly she liked helping Little Jack. Despite her unusual paranormal ability, she felt overpowered and vulnerable due to her need for visual contact, highlighted in some conflicts in the past.

Suddenly, Osa pointed towards a valley and a clearing. "I see it. The hacienda is down there. You're good on the plan?"

"Yes. Is here good? I see the edge of the trail. To the house, it's about a mile, just over."

---

[14] In the comic book "Special Operations – the War Years" # 1 (Jan 2023 release)
[15] See TM 4.4 "No Ifs, Ands, or Butts

They were on a very old, paved road that looked like it had been built in the 1960s and never touched since. The road lacked striping and had no shoulder, weeds and trees growing right up to the edge. The road led to a road that eventually took the user into Madrid, but here they were in a remote area of the country. There were homes in the distance, but the hacienda was unique. The trail was a simple bike trail, dirt and winding through the undergrowth. This was to be Osa's route to the hacienda.

"Yes. Any questions on the plan?" asked Osa.

"No. Just be sure to remember the code words," said Joy nervously.

"Timing?"

"Fifteen minutes. I have 12:03," said Joy, checking her watch by holding it up at an angle to protect the glare from the sun. The day was sunny and hot, about ninety degrees, fairly typical July weather in Madrid.

"Same," said Osa. "Radar, are you linked in?"

"I am. I've got two robots midway, so whoever runs into trouble first I'll be there," said Radar.

Radar had uncovered a potential Society-owned property in Sitges, about an hour away, that might have value to raid while Osa and Joy were securing Tonya Duncan at the hacienda. One of the Radar robots and Lisa McGrath were going there. Sherry and Little Jack were raiding a warehouse in Madrid.

"I hope you just sit on your ass and rust," said Osa.

"Me, too. Good luck, ladies."

Joy quickly stopped and Osa hopped out. The road was barely wide enough for two vehicles and had a lot of blind curves thanks the foliage, so Osa didn't mess around. She simply said, "Good luck."

"You, too."

Osa jumped out and headed up the trail quickly. The plan was relatively straightforward. Radar's reconnaissance indicated only three household members — Fred and Jill guarding Tonya. But it was out of date and his last check distorted by Tonya's aural disguise spell. Unaware Tonya had left for Sitges, Joy was posing as a lost businesswoman. They knew Tonya would never answer the front door, so Joy would ambush whichever security person answered and use that person to take out the other.

Meanwhile, Osa could get to the rear of the hacienda via the trail and would serve as backup. If things went well, she wouldn't have much to do.

Well, things didn't go well.

Osa was halfway to the house when she heard on Joy's com, "Hey, look out!"

Then there was a horn, then a thump, then Joy screamed.

"Joy? Joy!" shouted Osa, pausing in her walk.

Then Osa heard noise, a Spanish speaking male. Osa had no choice. She couldn't leave Joy on her own. Osa turned to run back to the road.

The problem was, the hacienda had a third security member, which no one didn't knew about, because she arrived at the last minute, literally minutes after Radar's final aural sweep. As Osa neared the road and crouched to see if Joy had been in an accident or ambushed, she felt a gun stick in her neck.

"Move or channel and I blow your brains to Libya."

Osa very slowly raised her hands and raised from her crouch behind the large oak tree in the three-foot tall weeds along the side of the road. She felt the cold nuzzle of a gun barrel on the back of her head, where her hair met her neck. She tested her channeling, and her aura was blocked, so whoever had the gun on her was also paranormal.

"Uh, easy, lady, I'm sorry if I was trespassing," said Osa, trying to sound stupid and innocent.

The woman had a hint of a Spanish accent but spoke excellent English. "Don't play coy with me, Carerra."

"Ah," said Osa, now recognizing the voice, which made her very nervous. "I won't do anything foolish, Paula. You know self-preservation is my game."

"Perhaps. Hands behind your back."

Osa complied. Quickly, she felt cuffs going around her wrists. Her stomach tightened. This was a total fucking mess.

"Can I turn around so we can talk? I'm sure we can cut a deal," said Osa hurriedly.

"Turn."

When Osa turned, she saw thirty-eight-year-old Paula de Costa. She had very short-cut black hair, bright blue eyes, a classic profile, and a tall frame. She was pretty, but in a cold manner, almost as if she were a cold version of Osa.

Osa knew Paula from their Society days. When Osa was revealed as a double-agent, Paula took it hard. Osa had gleaned a lot of information over the years from Paula.

Osa tested her channeling again, but obviously de Costa had strong aural blockers in place. Osa could feel her channeling, but it would take an effort to channel. But that wasn't an immediate problem. She knew Joy's crash and her capture would alert the robot Radars, who would be at the property in just a few minutes.

"Paula, if you wanted me dead, I'd be dead. So, let's talk terms."

Paula smiled like a shark finding fresh blood. "I set the terms and you surrender. That's what we talk about. Come. Into the car."

Osa grimaced and walked to the car, now parked on the road at the end of the trail, a black Bentley. Paula placed her inside the car into the rear passenger seat, shoving Osa back on her handcuffed hands. The car had plexiglass separating the front and back. There were no openings from the inside. Basically, it looked like a police car.

"Have you hurt Joy?"

"Shut up." Paula shoved her hard into the car, causing Osa to wrench her shoulder.

"Ow, that hurts," muttered Osa.

"Get used to it."

Once they were on the road, Osa asked, "How far are we going? I like music on road trips."

Paula turned, glared at her and said, "I have gags."

"Let's talk terms then. Why are you kidnapping me? What do you want?"

"I don't want anything. My employer does."

"Tonya."

Paula nodded.

"Fine. I want to talk to her as well," said Osa, not in a sassy way, but as if they were equals conversing instead of captor and captive.

"That won't happen for a while, Osa. Nighty-night."

"Awwww, c'mon . . . I hate . . . gasssssss," moaned Osa, and within seconds she was out cold.

Paula quickly drove down the road for the main gate. Walking to the house from the trail would have been hard carrying Osa. It was much easier to drive the half mile with Osa unconscious.

At the driveway, Fred said, "We've got the blonde as well. She got in a freak car accident, missed a curve and ran into the ditch, which saved us the trouble of knocking her out."

"Okay, let's move," snapped Paula. "They'll make good hostages, because I'm sure we're going to be visited shortly by their big gun."

"Big gun?"

"Radar."

Chapter Seven
The Waterless Water Park

"Fun place," said Radar sarcastically as he and Lisa stared at the entrance to an aquatic park that had closed more than twenty years ago. The endless water slides, water rides, and paths had been the home of taggers and airsoft players, but Tonya had purchased the property via Interwtine in 2018 and run them off. However, it still looked the same. Everywhere there were weeds, broken rides and slides, and endless graffiti that made the place look like a child's chalkboard. It was also very dangerous, because there was a lot of cover for assailants and the layout was difficult to follow because some rides were completely gone, others damaged, other relatively intact, so keeping one's bearings straight was difficult.

The slides had all long ago been stripped off and were just shells. There was garbage everywhere. The piping showed and all the ponds were dried and cracked concrete casings.

Leaving the park abandoned and dilapidated served Tonya's interests, because the park had a large underground area that the Consortium had used for some paranormal experiments and as holding areas for torture victims. Presently, though, it was between projects.

"Fun? Really? I always thought water parks were stupid," said Lisa. She stood with her hands on her hips, her body normally long and lanky and appearing more so given she was wearing gray Kevlar and had her hair in a ponytail. "It looks like shit."

Radar chuckled. Being a robot, he didn't need protective clothes. He wore jeans and a black hoodie with ancient, brown boots. He was walking cautiously behind a triple water slide that ran to an empty pool. The overgrown brush didn't do much to hide him.

"Hey, at least we got in for free."

"Just because something is free doesn't mean it's a bargain," said Lisa wryly. "That's McGrath economics 101."

"Hold on," said Radar, studying what appeared to be a wristwatch on his right wrist. It was actually an infra-red and motion sensor that was linked to other paranormal apps. Paranormals could screen their aura, but nothing could screen them from the heat detector app . . . or Radar's robotic hearing. "I've got two. They're in what had been a restaurant. One is definitely Tonya. Fuck! She's pulled something and fooled my reconnaissance."

"You sure?"

"Yeah. Her aura is blocked, but I beat her blockers. The other isn't paranormal, probably a hostage or a victim."

"Then let's do something."

"We gotta be careful. You go around the other side, and we go in together."

Lisa moved off. Radar adjusted his hearing. Homing in on the inside conversation was not possible. There was too much background noise and the restaurant's walls were still intact, though covered in graffiti and bird-droppings. But he was hearing occasional screams.

Then an alarm sounded.

"Fuck. Move Lisa! I'm gonna be busy."

"Dad, I think we're going to be busy," said Jill as she watched the feed from a drone that was a remarkable replica of a morning dove, sitting in a tree near the main gate.

Fred leaned over his daughter's right shoulder as she sat at her station in the security room, a small room near the front door. He hit the console and said, "Damn. You're right. Are Osa and Joy secure?"

"Yes, they're both knocked out and tied up in the wine cellar. Paula is headed back to Sitges to help out Tonya."

"Fine. Then let's use the old Soloman's Ridge tactic."

Jill looked up and smiled. "I like that one. Any need to keep our attackers alive?"

"Nope."

"Death is your end game. Make it easy," said Tonya a few minutes earlier as she watched her victim writhe in the restaurant, still whimpering from her latest torture. Blood rolled out of her right ear, and the icepick Tonya had shoved into it was still embedded.

Finally, Helena opened her eyes and glared. That was about all she could do, because she was bound to a wooden X-frame with chains, arms and legs spread, her aura blocked and thus helpless. A twenty-three-year-old from Kiev, she had light skin, dark eyes, and a jutting chin. Her hair was long and black, and her frame lithe with obviously artificial breast enhancement. Nude, she was sweating. The room itself was quite hot, for it was concrete with nothing but a bench holding instruments of torture and a black swivel chair borrowed from an upstairs office, but she was also scared.

Tonya smiled like a hunting cheetah. "You're going to suffer and die, because I need answers and TM power. But how much you suffer is dependent on your answer to my single question. I'm losing patience. Do you understand?"

Helena nodded slowly. Once. Glaring.

"Where is Laura Jabbar?"

Helena immediately shook her head and shut her eyes.

"Ah," said Tonya, as if a cat had peed on the rug. She removed the gag. "Well, that is disappointing. Of course, it's a woman's prerogative to change her mind, so you may want to remember that when the pain becomes unbearable."

Helena braced herself.

Tonya's voice was sing-song, as if talking about some far away time and place. She stroked Helena's body as she spoke, pausing to pinch the victim's nipples once, but mostly just rubbing and making it quite clear to Helena that Tonya now owned her body.

"I'm not a monster nor am I Laura's enemy," said Tonya slowly. "I know that a little hard for you to believe, but both are true. My mother was a paranoid schizophrenic. She would beat me to the point I couldn't get out of bed, cut me, burn me. I was always beat up. No one liked me. I didn't do well in school. She finally snapped and sliced my father with a butcher's knife like fifty times. She's in an institution now for the criminally insane."

She paused. Helena glared, certain this was a ploy. She didn't believe anything Tonya was telling her, though in fact it was all completely true.

Pausing to grab Helena by the hair, Tonya said, "Look at me when I speak to you, understand?"

Helena grunted.

Tonya let her hair go and said, "As soon as I turned 18, I left Oregon and headed for San Diego. I wanted to go somewhere warm and happy. And there I started work at the Box, at Meridian. I rose to the top. I had a lover, Lamar. God, I loved that man. He was bisexual. Lord, we had fun there. I don't remember all of it, but I do remember it was all fun."

She smiled, looking genuinely happy.

Then she turned cold. "It was there I learned about the Society. It was there I learned about being part of something larger, about being part of an organization that would change mankind, save mankind. I have devoted my life to the Society. I have done so many things to help save this planet and people that it's beyond your feeble comprehension."

Tonya slapped Helena hard quickly, twice, once on each cheek. Helena didn't react, but it hurt, though it was nothing compared to the pain in her ear.

"You are an insolent slut. Laura is a traitor. She will die. No doubt you think keeping your information will protect her. It won't. it will only make you suffer more."

Tonya now stepped in front of Helena and whispered, "Prepare."

Helena looked defiant, but she was scared. She was not going to betray Jabbar, that was for sure.

Or so she thought.

Slowly, Helena realized it was getting dark in the room. At first, she assumed it was an automatic dimmer.

Then she realized her vision was slowly vanishing in her right eye.

She began to panic and twist in her chains. She screamed, the scream that alerted Radar outside.

Tonya chuckled. "Such bravery." Pause. "But you're right to be terrified. You see, I am an exceptional TM, but I'm also an elemental channeler. I can control water at a level most channelers cannot. I can manipulate it without visual contact, meaning I can move it around *inside* the body."

Slowly, the vision in Helena's left eye started to slowly vanish as well. She squeaked, and Tony laughed.

"Such a child. I'm putting fluid pressure on your optic nerve. Once it's destroyed, your vision is gone. And I can do the same to your eardrums, your nostrils . . . push your water to your bowels and give you endless diarrhea . . . I have quite the repertoire of tricks."

Helena was now blind.

"So, remembering it's a woman's prerogative to change her mind, and considering that the brain is about seventy percent water, what about Laura?"

Helena knew she had information that could buy her a quick death. But she knew nothing could buy her freedom, and as a result, she took a deep breath and said, "Do what you want. I can't help you."

Tonya put her right hand on Helena's forehead and her left hand between Helena's breasts. "Oh, you shouldn't hold out. You'll only cause yourself so much pain."

Tonya began to channel. Helena slowly began to feel a throbbing in the back of her neck, then her head. It got worse and worse and worse, as if she were being burned alive.

"Aghhhhhhhhhhhhhh!" she finally screamed.

Tonya said, "This is just the start. I'm moving around the water in your brain and spinal column. I'm destroying your body, Helena, and you're letting me do it for nothing. Nothing at all."

Helena cried.

Tonya smiled. "Don't be a baby. Just tell me things."

Helena said nothing and looked away.

Tonya channeled. "I'm putting pressure by adding fluid to your spinal cord. Try to move your feet."

Helena realized she couldn't. The thought of winding up paralyzed at the hands of this woman made her resolve crumble. "Wait. Stop!"

"You have something to say? Talk fast, then I stop."

"I know where Jabbar is."

"Where?"

When Tonya heard the answer, she was stunned.

But before she could react, the alarm on her phone sounded, alerting her to Radar's presence.

Helena noted the sudden change in Tonya's manner and expression, coughed, and realized she could move again. "Trouble in . . . paradise, Duncan?"

"A minor matter," said Tonya, but her eyes were fixed on the details being sent to her phone by the alarm.

"The alarm was in that direction," said Jill to her father, pointing through the window towards a restored blue 1970 VW van.

Fred took the binoculars from her. "Hmmmmmmmmm."

"The drone is also sending back surveillance pictures," said Jill, calling them up on her phone.

The site was incongruous. There was a white man with grayish brown, curly hair, a very tall man at six-five, one probably somewhere in his fifties. He was standing with the rear of the VW bus open. Jim Croce tunes were playing from the van. He was parked on a dirt road that loped the property. It met the main road, but he was up a few dozen yards from that.

"What's that fool up to? He must know we'll know it's him," said Jill, puzzled.

Fred continued to eye the van with his binoculars.

They suddenly screamed and threw themselves to the floor as they were hit with a vicious sonic wave.

Fred went down, but he was an elemental as well as a TM. He channeled and blew wind that blew through the hallway and the room, slamming the pair of them out through the window into the daisy-filled flower bed below.

Jill got to her feet first, covered in mud, and turned and said, "What was that?"

"What?"

"WHAT WAS THAT?"

Before Fred could answer, he turned and sent earth through the window.

A second Radar robot sent it right back.

Fred dove behind a small brick retaining wall, then took off running across the yellow field, the weeds in the area having died off due to lack of rain. They were outside the sprinkler line of the property.

Jill saw her father run and knew he was drawing Radar off. When the robot Radar jumped down to the grass and took off after her father, Jill prepared to blast him with bricks from a stone wall being bult nearby, hopefully cracking it like an eggshell.

But she had forgotten about the original Radar, the one dickering with his VW van.

"Hey, lady, got a light?"

Jill turned in horror, but she was way too late. Radar's shot a taser-like charge at Jill. She was hit in the left side as she turned. She cried out and yelped.

By the time she hit the ground, Jill was out cold.

VW Radar quickly pulled off his belt, which was really thick rope, and began binding Jill as he said, "Just a rainy night in Georgia, kid!"

Uphill, the other robot Radar was pursuing Fred. This was a gigantic mismatch, for the robot Radar could run a two-minute mile and Fred wasn't exactly the picture of health.

Quickly, Fred realized he was in big trouble. He ducked behind a large eucalyptus tree in a grove of apple trees and a couple of oak trees. Cicadas called at them. So did the birds.

Fred channeled his TM by disrupting the earth under Radar to hurl him in the air. But Radar was ready for that trick and rolled away. As he did so, he undid his right hand and fired a taser at Fred.

Fred, unlike his daughter, was ready and dodged, ducking behind the tree. But while he dodged, Radar unleashed another sonic blast.

"Arghhhhhhhh!" cried Fred, throwing his hands over his ears and falling to the ground.

Outside, the sonic blast was dispersed much more than in the house, but at this range it was still close enough to make Fred unable to cope.

Radar quickly closed in and injected Fred with a knock-out drug.

"Nice work, self!" said the Radar that had taken down Jill.

They gave each other high-fives and the Fred-stopping Radar said, "We're the best team out there. Let's get them inside and secure. You have a hit on Osa and Joy?"

"No, but I read body heat in the wine cellar. I don't detect anyone else here. We're secure."

"I can see through a hole on this side of the restaurant. Duncan is inside with a victim tied to a cross. Do we go in?" hissed Lisa into the com.

Radar turned to find five men in commando garb shooting at him. "Get in there!"

"I can't hear you!" shouted Lisa.

"They're shooting at me, hold on!" Radar shot a sonic wave at the men, which dropped them almost instantly. They rolled around with their hands over their ears.

"Idiots. I'm not a Buick. I'm completely bulletproof. Lisa, go in now!"

Lisa used her TM to telekinetically hurl logs that used to line the path at the weakened side wall, knocking a hole in it. She raced to it, used it for cover, and glanced inside.

Radar simply walked to his wall and kicked it in with his robotic strength.

Tonya had been alerted by a motion detector that Radar had missed because it was concealed in a drone that flew around like a bird. Radar had easily found and used disabling pulse wave on the other, but it missed the bird.

Moving quickly, Tonya sent a knife across the room with TK and slit Helena's throat. She didn't need that distraction and believed she could easily defeat her attackers without needing a hostage.

Prepared, Tonya now used a head detector app and saw Lisa outside the restaurant on her side. Radar had turned off his human sensory abilities, so he no longer registered on a heat app, but Tonya knew they would try to pincer her.

The second the two agents attacked, Tonya struck back. She stood in the middle of the restaurant, which was a perfect square, enabling to enhance her power through geometric channeling.

Lisa paused outside, but she was within range of Tonya's unique form of elemental channeling. Tonya gestured with her right hand and began drawing the water out of Lisa's body.

"Ghakkkkkkkkkk!" croaked Lisa as she suddenly felt like she was on fire. Within seconds, she would be dead.

But Radar wasn't as susceptible to this type of attack from Tonya. Tonya recognized Radar and knew he was a robot. But she also knew to pass as human, he had water in his makeup.

She pulled.

But Radar attacked, running across the room even as she was attacked.

Tonya had to disable Radar before he reached her. If he were human, she could have.

But he wasn't.

Panicked, she stopped her dehydration attack on Lisa and focused on Radar, saving Lisa's life.

Too late.

Radar slammed into her like a blitzing linebacker sacking a quarterback right after the pass. Tonya was slammed into the floor and crushed under Radar's weight, but the real damage was a blow to the back of her head, which hit the now concrete floor.

Tonya was out.

Radar slowly got up. Lisa staggered inside and said, "Jesus, I feel like I've been flash-fried. Is she dead?"

Checking Tonya's vitals, Radar said, "No, but she's not in good shape." Blood seeped from under Tonya's head. "We can't help whoever is on the cross. Let's try to get her out of her and see if we can save her."

"I'd rather just let her die," said Lisa grimly. "Unless that will send me back to Hell. What do you think?"

"Can't help with the metaphysical, kid, but she might have info. And in this state, luckily for us, she can't kill herself."

"Poison," said the VW van Radar over a com-link to Medina in Vegas a few minutes later. "I went to check on my robot self that took down Fred, came back, she was dead. They had it hidden in a masterful place, a fake lining on the roof of the mouth. Can't see it without a body scan. They used the tongue to undo it, then swallow the pill."

"I take it Fred took the same exit?"

"Yep, he did a Kevorkian, too."

"Shit. Okay, learn what you can there. Any word from your robot in Sitges?"

"Yeah, just got word. They found a victim dead. Tonya hit her head and looked to be in bad shape. Lisa and my third self are taking her to a WSA compound."

"Okay. Have you found Joy or Osa yet?"

"No. That's our next move."

"Okay. Keep me posted."

Radar one turned to Radar two and said, "Any reading?"

"Yeah. The aural blockers around the house suddenly turned on. I'm guessing there was a third person inside that ran for it. Come on. I get readings for both Joy and Osa, and the med baselines are perfectly normal."

"Hot damn. Our lucky day."

They raced inside the hacienda and through a kitchen to a small sitting room with a table and a sewing machine on it. Tied to chairs were Joy and Osa. Joy was still unconscious. Osa was coming around.

"Radar?" she muttered. "You look fuzzy."

"Hold still," said Radar one, freeing Osa while Radar two did the same for Joy. Both women had been lazily bound with rope and were easy for Radar to free by using a switchblade that could extend from the index finger on each robot.

"Did you get them all?" asked Osa, wincing as she had a bad headache, a side effect from the knockout gas.

"We took out two TMs, Fred and Jill, and they chose the suicide option," said Radar one.

"Joy's okay, just knocked out with a drug," said Radar one.

"Good," said Osa. "Where's Paula?"

"Who?"

"Paula de Costa. She's a TM I knew from Society days. She got the drop on me. As I was slowly coming around, she took off, maybe five minutes ago."

"I'll search," said Radar two.

Radar one asked Osa, "You okay?"

"Yah, just a headache. As I was coming around, Paula called someone. From what she said, she was fleeing the country. Big chicken."

"Well, if we don't find her now, we'll find her later. For now, we need to see if Tonya makes it, and if we can learn anything."

Chapter Eight
The History of Sex Channeling
July 5, 2021

"Tonya is in a deep coma. They don't think she'll ever come out of it, and if she does, she's almost certain to have brain damage," said Sam the next morning, which was July fourth in Las Vegas. They were in Medina's office at Ops' headquarters in Vegas at 8:03 the next morning. The robot Radars and Osa were at Radar's Berlin insurance company headquarters, where it was around dinner time, for a checkup. Joy and Lisa had gone back to the McGrath group's headquarters. The Vegas Radar was attending this meeting via a video link. He was sitting in the parking lot of the MGM Grand, sitting on a wall looking like he was playing with his phone.

"Well, that's great," said Medina glumly.

She and Sam were dressed casually. Medina wore gray pants that faded to black at the bottom with a yellow blouse with the buttons fastened down the middle to the neckline. Sam wore black running pants, white sneakers, and a purple Milwaukee Brewers' T-shirt. The air conditioning was already on. Vegas was in for another typical 105-degree summer day. At the casino, Radar wore a gray T-shirt with an American flag, black running shorts, and white sneakers.

"I don't know if it's that bad. I don't know that she could have helped us anyhow," said Radar thoughtfully. "She wasn't part of the original Morrison spell. I doubt she knew anything important, or anything much beyond what I hacked."

"Who was the woman Tonya killed?" Medina asked.

"Helena Gib-something. She was Society. Likely, she was working for the cabal trying to overthrow them from within, because she'd been tortured with an icepick through the eardrum and blinding, not some sort of BDSM stuff," said Radar.

"Okay. Enough with them. Let's focus on what we do know," said Sam.

"Right, Sam. First, Little Jack and Sherry's mission was a bust. The warehouse was cleaned out, probably weeks ago. Second, when my robots were at the hacienda, they got some info by hacking Tonya's emails. Everything Calico recorded is too secure, but Tonya got a little lazy and had a couple Consortium emails in her Intertwine work email that helped me figure this out. There are a couple side comments on an email to Sunset and Morgana's production company about anal sex, which is usually what is used in this thing I'll explain in a second — Tonya apparently was big into butt-games. This thing I uncovered turned out to be that the method used to instigate the spell in Tiera del Fuego, this being something called, well . . . sex channeling."

"I've never heard of that," said Medina.

"Here, read the emails."

They glanced at them. Medina said again, "Well, again, I've never heard of this, and I've heard of a lot of weird shit. You'd be surprised what goes on in a sorority at Wellesley."

"Me either," said Sam. "I mean, there's an index for it in the Ops files, but it says it was probably dropped from common practice, if it ever existed, centuries ago."

"Right. Which is what I knew as well, and I can search a lot better than you. Which means the fact that the art is lost and was found by NDE indicates to me nothing *conventional* is going to get us any answers," said Radar grimly.

"True enough," said Sam ruefully.

Medina frowned. "So, you did get one clue, the comment that it's anal. It's not something crazy."

"That's an assumption," said Sam.

Medina shook her head. "I don't think so. If it's an ancient art, it had to be invented before people had stuff like sex toys and the internet to develop deviant practices."

"Doesn't mean it can't be deviant," said Radar. "Could be sex with pigs, something like that."

"That wasn't the way she indicated, though," said Sam thoughtfully.

"I agree," said Radar.

"I think we're onto something — although what we can do with it, I don't know," said Radar.

Medina pouted. "Me, either."

Sam frowned. "There has to be a way to get info on this. If the Consortium did it, we can do it. Hell, we've gone to, uh, Hell and come back. Twice!"

Medina suddenly wagged her finger at Sam. "You know . . . we learned with that Quotient stuff the Bible has a lot of significant references to paranormal events. What if there's a clue there?"

"In what way?" asked Sam.

Medina shrugged. "Damned if I know, but if we're talking anal, maybe the story of Sodom and Gomorrah?"

Sam shrugged and wiggled his hand to indicate a lukewarm enthusiasm. "I guess it's worth a shot." He paused and added, "We should call Tripper as well. He's older than dirt. Maybe he's heard something over the years?"

"Sure, why not? I'm sure he's sitting on his ass doing nothing."

"Gol' damn phone rings at the worst fuckin' times," muttered Tripper as he slid out from under his '86 Ford F150 on a wheeled bench. He had it parked in the alley behind his business, the Tricky Dick Detective Agency in Tupelo, Mississippi. Tripper was checking the shocks after a nasty up and down due to a pothole on I-22.

Tripper was now about 124-years-old, give or take. He stood six feet and six inches tall, looking like someone stretched too fast in a taffy twister. His bones were obvious through his rail-thin frame, but most people didn't notice because he tended to wear bulky clothing. Today he was wearing typical dress — jeans and a white T-shirt stained with coffee. He sported a mop of unruly, uncombed black hair buried under a ratty Atlanta Braves baseball cap, an untrimmed black beard, and dark-rimmed black glasses typical of the military — function over fashion. His wooden cane was carved into the shape of the head of a cottonmouth snake, and these days was mostly for show. The flask it held was useful and occasionally it helped channel a spell, but the cane was primarily to help channel his unique form of geometric channeling. Besides that, it threw opponents off guard, giving him the element of surprise in combat.

Tricky Dick Detective Agency was simply Tripper's cover used to uncover paranormal problems such as torture magicians. Tripper himself was an elemental channeler, which was the most common type of paranormal; an elemental could telekinetically control the ancient Greek elements earth, wind, air, and fire. But these days, Tripper mostly used geometric channeling, which was the use of geometric shapes to exponentially increase channeling power.

Tripper was preparing for a trip to Europe, to help with a vision Radar had about Russia, so he had gone to Memphis to see his assistant, friend, and lawyer, Cinnamon, before he left. On his return, he hit the pothole.

Once he was sitting up with his back leaning against the wall, he said, "If'n it ain't old Medina Kane! Reckon y'all must be up to y'all's panties in shit to be calling me at 6:30 in the morn your time."

"Nah, I just like your cheery voice. Sam is here, too, and Radar's on com-link."

"Hi, Sam. Reckon y'all work more now that y'all retired than ya did as field ops director."

Sam laughed. "It seems that way on days like this. Of course, this fourth of July is a lot fucking better than the *last* one!"

They all laughed at that. Last July 4, Sam had been framed by the Consortium Quartet member Amy Dayne, who was masquerading as Presidential candidate Shy Strong, and turned Sam into Public Enemy Number One, sending him on the run for months.[16]

"Radar, still patrolling the internet, I take it. What can a fine southerner like me help y'all with? I was just dickin' with my truck, but it ain't nothing important."

"Welllllll . . . it's a little kinky," said Medina suggestively.

Tripper chuckled. "Don't be teasing me, Medina. Y'all ain't too old for a spanking."

She laughed. "Yeah, but not from you. What are you, 150?"

"That's cruel, woman," he said, and he laughed. "What can I help you with?"

She explained what had happened in Tiera del Fuego and what Radar had learned. Then she asked, "We thought that, you know, since you've been around since dirt was invented, you might know something?"

"Yeah, reckon I've heard of it, but it's a lotta bull. It was real popular in the 60s and 70s as a way t'get dumb chicks to drop their panties. Ain't got a real whit of real channeling to it that I've found. All bullshit."

Clearly disappointed, Medina said, "Really? Nothing?"

"Nope. But I'd contact Golden Bear. He's got access to a lotta secret paranormal shit that Lexx gathered and that they've had in Russia through normal means since World War II. It may be some shit he ain't ever reckoned would be important."

"We'll try that," said Medina. "Thanks."

"Not a problem. I'll bill y'all for the consult."

"Consult? You didn't know anything!" she said, then she laughed.

"I'll knock off thirty percent. Call me if y'all want me to try and look into it, but I'll be headin' over to Europe to help out in a few days."

"Will do," said Medina, and she hung up. Then she looked at Sam. "What time is it in Moscow?"

Radar said, "They're like nine or ten hours ahead. Call his old ass."

***

---

[16] In TM 3.8 "Who am I?"

Golden Bear was watching a British sitcom about two old people in a nursing home when the phone rang. He was sitting in an ancient apartment near the Kremlin in Moscow, his bare feet up on the coffee table covered in stains, eating unbuttered popcorn. This was a rare relaxing moment for him, given the increasing tensions within Russia due to Putin's paranormal research.

He was 101 years old but looked about sixty thanks to a combination of healing spells and glamours, which were how a TM was able to alter his or her base appearance and look older or younger. He was tall and gaunt, but emanated power. He had more wrinkles than a mountain range, and multiple age spots on his skin. His eyes were icy blue, almost white, and his teeth were dentures. Despite a prominent nose, he was probably attractive in his youth. His hair had mostly vanished, but there was a small, long ring left around the edge of his skull, all white. He was about six feet and eight inches tall, and his arms and legs were skinny. Wearing old brown slacks, a yellow and black checkered shirt, and boots, he looked like someone having just stepped out of a retirement home.

Golden Bear was the ultimate Russian hero. He'd been on the team with Tripper that killed Hitler in '45. But in the late 1990s, Golden Bear more or less vanished. In 2016, after years of searching, Tripper found his old friend hiding out in Siberia working for the alien Lexx, who was running the Consortium. After that, Golden Bear had returned to Atlantia with Queen Marrina, Lexx, and others. There, they had been working at helping Lexx return to his home planet, among other things. But after Marrina was killed, Golden Bear returned in late 2017 to Russia to start to create Russian Special Ops. That had hit a snag when it was found Calico and Englehart had infiltrated the group. He was still trying to pick up the pieces.[17]

"Ah, Miss Kane. Good to talk to you. What is your pleasure?"

"Well, I'd like about ten billion dollars and early retirement, but I'd settle if you could tell me about sex channeling."

---

[17] See TM 3.1 "Escape"

Oddly, he was quiet for a moment. Then he said, "It very old, very arcane art. All knowledge of it lost long ago. Where you learn about it?"

"Well, I haven't. That's the point." She explained for him.

"Ah," he said thoughtfully, his popcorn forgotten. "I know nothing, though I must, how you say? Research files. In fact, I not know any person who know anything."

Disappointed, Medina said, "Someone must know something. The Consortium found out."

"How?"

She said, "One of their dudes had a shitload of NDEs and came back with the info. Or so our information says."

He paused before saying, "Then there is your answer."

"Huh?"

"You must find this man."

"I don't know that we can, and even if we do, he won't tell us," said Medina. "He's the cause if this whole mess."

Golden Bear laughed heartily. "Ah, but he not *source* of info."

"No, the dead told him . . . aw, fuck, nothing like missing the obvious," said Medina.

"Da. You must, how you say?"

"Contact the dead?"

"Take out the middleman. You must contact dead and find out who knows."

"I lost the phone number to Hell and Heaven. You happen to have it?" she asked.

"No, but the others know how to contact the dead. It not easy, and carries grave risks, but it can be done." He laughed. "I send you names and references." He laughed heartily. "I get finder's fee."

Medina whistled. "Okay, thanks. Well, you go back to your dinner or whatever."

"Popcorn. I will dig into files, but don't, how you say? Hold your panties."

"Hold your breath."

"I like mine better," he said, laughed, and hung up.

Medina hung up as well. Sam had politely listened in, as had Radar. Radar said, "We seem to be rocketing to nowhere in a hurry."

"Tripper knows the Voodoos, obviously. Maybe he can contact them while we work on finding Morrison and checking the references Golden Bear sends us. I mean, I know we're doing that, but I think now it has to be priority. I think that's a better bet," said Sam pragmatically.

"Yeah, we have to explore all options. If Tang was right about this 32-day thing, we're rapidly running out of time."

Chapter Nine
Dead Men Walking, Sort Of
July 6, 2021

"Glad y'all had time for the trip," said Tripper the next day at about nine in the morning.

"*This* is the place?" asked Medina skeptically as she, Sam, and Tripper approached a huge office building in downtown Austin, Texas.

"Yup. I done used Google," said Tripper, showing them his phone as Sam paid the Uber driver who had brought them from the hotel two blocks away.

Hands on hips, Medina stood looking up. The building was almost solid black, but the outer corners and rooftop corners had some sort of gray, metal shielding. The black didn't reflect light.

Medina bit her lip. She wore a light blue jacket and skirt over a white blouse with white hose and yellow heels. Sam wore a black suit and a purple and black striped tie. Tripper, well, was Tripper. He wore his typical jeans and Atlanta Braves cap. At least his T-shirt was clean.

"It looks like the sort of place Little Jack would've worked from before he became, ah, enlightened," said Sam.

"I checked with him, and he knew nothing about sex channeling or this place either. Thank God we had Golden Bear," said Medina.

They stood staring. The entrance was sunken from the main street down fourteen stairs and had six double-doors. There was an area of brush around the front and a large sign without an address but naming the building:

TIFFANY'S COMPLEX

"I reckon that sign sure knows a lot," said Tripper. "Anyone building this place and namin' it after themselves gotta have an ego the size of Trump."

Sam looked at her. "Well, into the lion's den?"

"Sure, what the Hell . . . uh . . . never mind," said Medina.

They entered the lobby, which resembled the lobby of a hotel. There were six booths, all with attractive brunette women manning the stations. To either side were escalators leading to a second lobby, and so forth. There was an elevator bay under the right escalator with a fake potted plant.

"Gee, are they clones?" whispered Medina to Sam.

Radar interjected. "They're good lookin', like a young Crystal Gayle."

"Down, boy," said Medina.

"Hey, I'm on com," he said, for he hadn't sent a robot body with them. "I can window shop."

Medina almost laughed, but held it in. She approached the station on the end, Sam flanking her rear right, Tripper her rear left. To the clerk, she said, "Uh, we have an appointment with Madam Maryvale."

The clerk smiled. "You're expected. Go on up. It's room 815. Take the elevator to floor eight and it's the first executive conference room on the right."

"Uh, thanks," said Medina.

They walked away. Medina whispered to the men, "This is a little weird, even for me."

"I seen weirder. Ever been to a cockfight in Ensenada?"

Medina just gave him a look.

"Well, that's weirder," said Tripper, making his point.

They rode up in silence as they had passengers with them. They reached the eighth floor. The floor was very quiet. There was thick, brown shag carpeting, tall oak doors, and security locks.

Medina paused before the door for 815 and knocked.

The door swung open to reveal an airy executive conference room that featured a view of downtown Austin, a huge rectangular glass table with seating for twenty, presentation boards on each side, and a huge aquarium full of large, blue fish. Plants hung from the ceiling, there was 80s music, and the temperature was perfect.

Standing before the door was Madam Terry Maryvale. She was thirty-eight with a very large bosom, butt, and chubby cheeks made bigger by a wide smile. She had curly brown hair and blue eyes. Sam thought she looked a bit like someone took Jennifer Saunders and Bonnie Kavanaugh and shoved them together into one body. Terry wore a lot of gold jewelry and a bright green jacket over a white bodice with a short black skirt and matching black hose. Her footwear was white booties.

Moving forward, she shook Medina's hand. "Miss Kane, an honor. I am Madame Terry Maryvale, conduit to the dead."

"Pleased. These are my, ah, assistants, Sam Grant and Tripper O'Sullivan."

"Charmed," said Sam with a smile. They shook.

"Pleased t'meet'cha," said Tripper with a quick shake.

"Well, come into the conference room. I cleared a couple hours for you. It's nice to have a client that has some cash to chase their desires to see the dead."

Terry stayed at the head of the table. Tripper sat on the side near the door, Medina and Sam across from them, Sam on Medina's right. They were cautiously protecting her as the leader.

"Place ain't a'tall what I expected, I reckon," said Tripper, looking around.

"What, did you think talking to the dead was still something done by creepy skanks in black skirts skulking around New Orleans in the dark eating shrimp?" she asked with a politely amused smile.

"Well, yeah, reckon so," said Tripper, then he laughed. "I been to Hell. I ain't never spent much time trying to talk to the dead."

"That's really a good philosophy," said Terry, cocking her head. "But I think you have an important mission here, from what your leader says."

"Yes, we need to learn about sex channeling. Unless *you* know something?" asked Sam warily.

Terry smiled. "I know a lot of things, but nothing about that. I've occasionally heard the dead talk about it, but not in a long, long time. See, reaching the long deceased is hard. It's like . . . well, it's like the cache in a computer memory. The long-dead aren't in the cache. It takes longer to reach."

"But it can be done?" asked Sam.

"Sure. But that's more than you need." She smiled. "Miss Kane, I run a very profitable business, and I like that. I have six homes in five different countries, cars, helicopters, a private jet, and more money than I could ever spend. Talking to the dead is big business."

"Desperation is big business," said Sam.

Terry winked. "You're onto something there." Then she turned back to Medina. "But I am after something very specific. I have talked to the dead since I was ten. And I do not want to be dead. There's ways around it. I use Soloman's Liquid, for I am a channeler."

"Ah, ha. I done knew there was a gimmick here. Y'all is a channeler that can key the aura of the dead and pull it down, right?"

Now Terry glared for a moment, then shrugged. "Sure. That's all I do. You're right." Then to Medina she said, "I want to make sure I live forever. So, I'll do this for you, but I want the guarantee from Ops of perpetual immunity and a perpetual supply of Soloman's Liquid on demand. I have my own supplies, but I want a backup."

"We don't keep it. We don't advocate that," said Medina.

"But you know where it is," said Terry pointedly. "And so now I will know where it is."

Medina glared at Terry, and for several seconds they were locked in a glare. Medina did not like the terms of this deal, but as Sam had said, more or less, they were desperate. "Fine. It's agreed."

"I want a verbal contract. Can we record it?"

"Sure."

That took several minutes. Once that was over, Terry said, "Okay, wait here for five minutes."

Medina frowned. "Sure."

"Y'all got a shitter?" asked Tripper.

"Down the hall to the left. The right is a gateway to Hell. Don't go there."

"Aw, gimme a break," said Tripper.

Terry laughed and exited.

Tripper went to the shitter, so Medina asked Sam, "What do you think?"

"I'm sure we're being recorded, so my thoughts shall remain my own," said Sam with a frown.

"Yeah, that's the way I feel."

"It's a nice office, nice view. But, you know, many a pretty façade has hidden a corrupt structure."

Medina snorted. "No kidding. I'm just annoyed I couldn't cut a better deal. I don't trust anyone that wants immortality."

"That's probably a valid concern, but we weren't in a position of strength. You did well," said Sam.

"Thanks."

Suddenly, Tripper returned. He made a face. "Place was cleaner than a Mr. Clean commercial. Creepy."

He sat and suddenly Terry returned. "I have your information."

Startled, all three of them sat up like eager schoolchildren. Medina said, "You're kidding?"

She waved a flash drive. "Nope. I put it on flash drive for you. That's easier. You can review at your leisure. If you like, I can set up a room here."

Medina frowned and took the drive. "We'll check it out later when we can review it in detail. It's a pleasure doing business with you."

Terry smiled. "Same. O'Sullivan, don't come back. The bathroom smells like shit."

***

"This is a load of shit, don't you think?" Medina asked Sam when they were outside.

"No. I think she wants what she wants, and if she can really read the aura of the dead, then getting what we want is no harder for her than us doing something like looking it up on the internet. She doesn't benefit by pulling a scam. That would just lead us to void the deal. Let's get back to the hotel and review it."

"Okay."

"Y'all, I reckon we gotta get some booze on the way. Ain't no point in learnin' if y'all ain't drunk while doing it."

Medina laughed. "I supposed Ops has to pick up the cost?"

"Sure as shit, Kane. Y'all is learning fast."

"So what did we learn?" asked Sam when they were back at the hotel and had reviewed the footage, which ran four minutes and two seconds. They uploaded it to Ops so Radar could view it as well, but they didn't have him active on a com-link.

Medina threw herself back on the bed on her back and groaned. "That there's merit in what they did and that we can do it, too."

They were in a Westin with a double bed, as Medina and Sam had planned to spend the night. Tripper would drive back to Tupelo when they were done. He was sitting on a chair around a circular table, playing with the ashtray in his hands. Sam sat on the second bed, leaning against the headboard, ice on his knees to help soothe the arthritic pains.

"Yeah, that's the main point," said Sam.

Tripper kept playing with the glass ashtray, as if it were a Rubik's cube he was trying to figure it out. "Reckon I got the gist of it. Tonya's emails mentioned t's usually anal, and we confirmed that. Sex channeling focuses on the anal so both men and women can use it."

"Let's walk back through it," said Sam. "Medina was right about one thing. There was a biblical tie-in. Sex channeling was used in ancient times and ended with the destruction of Sodom and Gomorrah."

"Y'all can't make assumptions. Reckon Tiffany might well have gone into the shitter and made this all up on the toilet," he said, putting down the ashtray.

"You don't believe that," said Sam.

"Nope. I reckon she's up-front. Okay, go on."

"In biblical terms, God visited Abraham and said he'd wipe out the city because of the people's sin, but he'd spare them if he could find ten people who were righteous. He didn't, and God put an ass-whipping on them, burning them down. Sodom was a vile place, and the main wickedness, to use the biblical word, was sodomy."

"Gay sex," said Medina.

Sam shook his head. "No, as Tiffany's source said, the wickedness was anal sex. And it wasn't wicked because of what it was, but because it gave them unnatural powers which they used to take advantage of others. The problem wasn't the sodomy. The problem was the channeling that came from the *sex channeling* triggered by the sodomy."

Medina sighed. "Well, we know what we have to do. Tiffany gave us the, uh, breakdown of the . . . positions and movements."

"Most of it is geometric," said Tripper.

"Yeah. I just have to find Ops agents who are willing to try it out."

Tripper chuckled. "Too bad ol' Grant there can't channel or you'd be all set. I reckon a man that could handle ladies like Bam and Meredith can damn well sex channel his way t'Hell an' back."

Sam smiled, knowing Tripper was saying this in jest, that there was no disrespect meant towards him or either of Sam's late lovers.

Medina said, "Are *you* in?"

"Reckon . . . well, I reckon the answer is yes and no."

"It's not that type of question," said Medina.

"Reckon it is, youngin'. You're in a new area, and that's not a department for a man pushin' one, two, five. I'll monitor, but I can't participate. I'm a big-ol' ways past the experimental sex age. It'd take me a couple days to get it up."

Sam laughed. "At least you still can."

"Yeah, if'n I got me some porn. Where y'all gonna be runnin' this spell from?"

"Not sure yet."

"Okay. I'm glad to help in other ways, but I gotta get back to Tricky Dick right now and get things settled there. Once I get back over to Europe, I ain't a gonna be back for a while."

"Sure. I'll text you the location when we're a go."

He rose, shook Sam's hand, and hugged Medina as he said, "Reckon that's be right. Meanwhile, y'all can send me any info y'all got and I'll start reviewing it. I'm pretty well done closin' off all my cases, wanted that done a'fore I went overseas."

"I'll send the info," said Medina. "Bye."

"Later, gator. Keep 'em hanging, Grant."

"You, too."

Once he left, Medina looked at Sam.

"Well, I guess we know we need four people for a square. I'd like more. But at least four. I can handle it, so we need three."

"You're really up for it?" asked Sam, arching an eyebrow.

"Ahhhhhh . . . sure. Just between us, Sam, I had a fun time at a lot of college parties. I wasn't always the mature head of Special Operations you see now."

Sam laughed. "I've heard as such from your sister."

Medina made a face. "Well, I guess I start with her."

Chapter Ten
Recruiting for the Counter-spell

Geneva answered simply, "Sister, even if I were not on a vital mission in Europe, I am married. There is no way I can do this."

"Why not?"

"You'll understand when you're married," said Geneva dryly.

"I think Lon would understand."

"Ah, well, like I said, you'll understand when you're married," said Geneva. "I'm sorry."

"It's okay."

"It was good to chat, though. Good to talk to you, too, Sam."

"Same here. We'll be talking again soon."

"I am certain. Have a nice afternoon. Is it afternoon where you're at? Regardless, have a good day."

"We will. You, too."

Medina terminated the call and looked at Sam. "Well, what now?"

"Experience counts."

"I know. I mean, this is a channeling none of us have ever used, so we're all new at it, but just the ability to handle emotions during this is gonna be important," she said, crossing her legs. "Let's get an early dinner and then start making calls. Deal?"

"If you're expensing it."

***

"Thanks for the free meal," said Sam as they sat at a quiet table in the corner of a Whataburger, the red and white roof and decor making Sam feel like he was inside a candy cane.

"You're welcome. Damn, I can tell we're in Texas. Look at the size of this meat! And the smell and taste."

"Try not to have an orgasm," said Sam dryly.

She laughed. "Aw, I'm the boss now. I couldn't do that."

Sam laughed.

Medina looked around, then whispered, "There is something I have been dying to know since I took over this job."

"How soon you can quit?"

"No. Did you and Bam or you and Meredith ever," and she made the universal finger gestures for sexual intercourse, "in your office?"

Sam actually blushed. "Not there, no. Not anywhere in any *official* building."

Medina nodded. "I figured as much. But I had to ask." Then she put a hand on his. "They were good women. I'm really sorry for your loss, Sam."

"Yeah. I wish it had worked out with Theresa, but we're just at very different points in our lives."

"Sometimes life is like that. I've had a couple guys that I thought maybe they were it. If there's a maybe, they aren't it. I'm glad Geneva found Lon. They're a good couple. Maybe I'll find that one day." She shrugged, took a bite, sipped her gigantic diet Pepsi, and said, "And maybe not. I don't care. I'm happy with who I am."

"That's the way to be."

She paused and said, "It's fun working with you."

"It's not hard having the old boss second-guessing you?"

She winked. "Hey, sis is always doing that. I've been used to that since I was six."

Sam laughed. "I can see that."

Medina rolled her eyes. "My sister is a great woman. I love her to death. Everyone loves her. But boy, she rides my ass like a cowboy with spiked heels. Always has." She laughed. "Not that I blame her. I was, shall we say, immature and irresponsible for much of my younger life." She laughed. "One time, this is like back in '17, I got in my head I was really gonna be a channeler and show her. She trained me for like an hour back home, and I think we wound up breaking some windows and she gave up in frustration and so did I." She smiled at the memory. "But I grew up. I just matured . . . differently."

Sam laned back. "I always felt like Geneva was born an adult, you know?"

Medina snapped her fingers. "That's it exactly! I must remember that. Anyhow, it's nice to talk with you." She paused and ordered desert. So did Sam. "Anyhow, what do the others think of me?"

Sam artfully dodged the question. "Hell, I hardly ever talk to the others these days. I mostly hang out with Jameson and we're like two old fucks in some 90s sitcom."

She laughed. "You should give that idea to Nicole. I bet one of her playwright friends could make it work."

He leaned forward and paused as their desert came. When the waitress left, he said, "They all like you. You connect with them well. That's the main thing."

"Thanks." She paused. "Sam, I have something I've been thinking about. I want to run it by you, but you have to promise not to laugh at me."

Seeing she was dead serious, he said, "Scout's honor. Does anyone know what that means these days?"

"Nope." She took a breathe, then ate a bite of her chocolate sundae. Then she said, "You know . . . let's talk about this back at the hotel. Is that okay?"

"Sure." She ate, then said, "I really want to talk, Sam. Nothing else. You got that, right?"

"Of course," he said, smiling gently. "I have no desire to have a relationship, Medina, but anyhow, our relationship is more like a mentor and mentee. I don't want to complicate that."

"Me either." She smiled and was obviously relieved. "You're a good man."

"Well, maybe. It depends on whether or not I laugh at your idea."

***

"So that's . . . that's the gist. Well?"

They were sitting at the table with the TV tuned to INN. Sam leaned back and whistled. "That's a big proposal."

Eagerly, she said, "I can make it work."

Sam put his hands behind his head and smiled. "You sure think big, I'll give you that. Do you have an actual plan or is this just a concept for the moment?"

"Mostly concept. But I think it would do a lot of good."

Sam shook his head. "I don't know. I can see the value of making Ops public. More and more, paranormal events are being recorded due to phones. I mean, Jameson never had to really deal with this shit. But you're also going to get every kook and tin-foil hat wearier who saw Martians steal his shoes heading for Ops."

Medina nodded. "I know that. But if Ops were public, we'd spend time really helping people and not pretending that, say, a weird experiment caused the 805 to ice over in San Diego."

He laughed. "I'll never live that one down, will I?"

"Not as long as there's an internet," she said, and laughed.

"Well, I will say that I believe there's merit to the idea. My main concern is the trauma center. Those people need privacy and safety."

Medina made a face. "Yeah, I hadn't thought of that."

"We could do something like split the campus. We should talk to Doc Keppel. Let's say we solve that. Getting it through is then a major political struggle. You think budget meetings are bad?"

She made a gagging sound, then said, "Oh, yeah."

"These are those meetings on steroids. It would be easier to get Tripper to throw out his fucking Atlanta Braves baseball cap than get this through. It would be easier to get Searly to have sex with a dog than to get this through."

"Oh, nothing is *that* impossible," said Medina. "But I take your point. How should I go about it?"

"Let's get guys like Carrington and McMichaels on our side. If they're in for it, we go to Shank. He's like a bad character in a Hemingway novel, but he has major political pull. Let's start putting together a plan."

"Us? You'll help?"

"Sure. Trust me, you'll need it. This is a major job. It's going to take a couple years."

"Really? Whoa."

"Well, it's not like we can just stop all crime to work on this," said Sam, laughing. "So, let's deal with our immediate problem first. We need recruits for our sex channeling event."

Medina nodded. "Yeah . . . not so easy. Okay, I'll start throwing names out. Searly?"

"You know her answer."

"Yeah. I'll call her and make it official."

"Uh, uh, no way. There's no way I'm doing that, guys. I don't know that it's safe for me to try new channeling with my whole 'Quafara gave me a stroke' thing in the first place, but even so, I couldn't do it. I'd freeze up and blow the whole thing."

Medina said, "That's what we thought, but we had to check."

"No problem. Good luck. I'm sure Sam knows some kinky chicks from Wisconsin who can help," said Searly, hanging up with a laugh.

After she hung up, Medina sighed. "We've some obvious exceptions. Radar's a robot. He's out. Mary isn't really a channeler, just a telepath. Chase . . . I don't even want to talk about her. None of the M-Men would be able to handle it."

"Probably not," said Sam. The M-Men were low-level channelers that helped hunt down totem users, vampires, and such in the Midwest. They weren't powerful enough to officially join Ops.

Medina said, "Let's try Nicole. I bet she'd do it just as a favor to me."

Sam shrugged.

"I don't know . . . if you're trying to get me naked, let me remind you you're my boss and that's sexual harassment, Miss Kane," teased Nicole.

"Duly noted. What's the answer?"

Nicole said unhesitatingly, "I'm in, but I'm not touching girls and no married men."

"Okay, that should work."

"I'm due back in Bolingbrook. I can buy some time, but not a lot, so let's get this done. Where and when?"

"I'll get back to you when I get enough people and confirm where they all are. We need four, right now it's me and you."

Nicole laughed. "I knew you were trying to get me naked."

She hung up.

Sam shrugged. "Well, you're up one."

"Yeah. I know who to call next."

From her parents' home in Centralia, Ashley McMillian said, "I think I can handle it. I'm intrigued by this form of channeling. I've never heard of it."

"It's a bit old-school. I'll send everyone who is in the group the info."

"Who else is there?"

"Well, I need one more."

"Well, forget the guys. Guys have a thing about taking it up the butt, think it makes them gay. You better call some girls, or at least some non-American guys."

"Thanks," said Medina. "Is Thunder around?"

"Yeah, he's about to leave. Hold on." Then a shout. "Thunder! Boss on the phone!"

Almost immediately, Medina was speaking with Thunder, John Bogut, who was staying with Ops' agent Ashley McMillian's parents while the two of them worked on helping Portland rebuild after Quotient destroyed it in September, 2020. Ashley had been born and raised there, and it served as a convenient base of operations for the two long-time Ops' partners and field agents.

"Crickey, Sheila, I was about to head over and see Gia," he said. Gia McKnight was a girl he'd met in Target in Centralia in 2020. They had a mostly 'friends with benefits' relationship, but Gia had also taken a role in helping the rebuilding of Portland. "Talk about timing."

"Time for sex, right? I need someone for a sex channeling spell."

"Sounds bloody fun, but I can't — not right now. I'm close on the trail of Andy Snyder, the TM. I can't stop. It could mean lives."

Seriously, Medina said, "I understand. You need help?"

"No . . . this is a job for a local guy. He's running a freemason's lodge. Thanks for asking, though. I'm sure you won't have any trouble finding takers. All Americans are sex maniacs," he said with a laugh. "Ashley is going, right? Ow!"

Ashley had been listening and socked him in the shoulder.

"You'd be surprised," said Medina dryly. "Later, Bogut."

"Tell Grant hello."

When Medina hung up, Sam said, "What about Joy or the McGrath Group girls? Little Jack's sisters?"

Medina gave him a look. "Hey, they just got back from Hell. Do you trust them?"

"For this, yes."

"Well, for what it's worth, so do I, but I figured Little Jack's Group we have to hold in reserve in case we mess this up and incinerate ourselves or let loose Godzilla or something like that," said Medina glumly.

Sam laughed. "Good points. Okay, what about someone who used to be with the Society? That might also give us information about this type of channeling that we can use."

Medina nodded and called.

"Uh, no. Sorry," said Bonnie Voodoo. "It's one thing to be a double-agent as a hat check girl. It's another to be in some sex orgy."

"It's sex channeling, and as a Voodoo you'd be great!" said Medina.

"Honey, it's not . . . I wouldn't be comfortable. I'm sure others will pitch in." There was a crash in the background. "The Waterfords are fighting," she said, referring to her two sisters and roommates. "I have to go. Bye."

Sam laughed. "Boy, you put her panties in a twist."

"Yeah, no shit. So will the next one."

***

Carrie Coleman said, "I'd do it, but I've been sick as a dog. If you need it within the next ten days, I'm out. I've got the flu. Otherwise, I'd give it a try."

"Yeah, we gotta move fast . . . maybe even tomorrow."

"Unless your sex channeling involves vomit, I'm out."

Sam said, "She's out."

Medina said, "Sorry, you're out. Feel better, hon."

"What about Osa?" asked Sam.

"I was saving her for last because she just got back yesterday from Spain, and no one is sure what gas was used on her in Spain. But Doc Morgan says she seems to be okay. I'll call her."

"My feeling is that this is *quite* an opportunity. What exact sexual acts are we talking about?" asked Osa with a sort of mix of seduction and amusement as she did a video conference with them five minutes later from her Vegas condo. She was wearing gray sweatpants, a white sleeveless T-shirt, and a yellow headband, having been running on the treadmill in the gym, trying to shake off jet lag. She was leaning against a wall with a jump rope ring next to it.

Medina made a face. "Well . . . more or less, you sit on a chair with a dildo up your butt while in a geometric square."

Osa shrugged. "I've done much stranger sex acts in the Society. Frankly, that's pretty tame. But I'd like to get something out of doing this other than a sore ass for a few days."

Medina laughed. "A raise?"

"Perhaps a company car?" suggested Osa.

"Blackmailer!"

"I can go join the WSA!" said Osa, teasing.

"Aw, fine, whatever." Medina said loudly, "Sam, see if Shank and the WSA have any used cars for sale."

"A *new* company car!" shouted Osa.

"Okay, okay, you're in. I'll text you time and place once we have the details."

"Sure. Talk to you later. I need to finish my workout. Nice to see you, Sam."

"Same. You're doing well?"

Osa winked. "I'm always good."

After she disconnected, Medina put up her hands for a high-five from Sam. "I did it!"

"Yeah," he said, laughing. "I guess Ashley was right about the guys."

"Nah, I just think we don't have many normal male agents right now. Anyhow, now we have to figure out where."

Sam shrugged. "I think speed and security are the most important. The counter-spell is only going to allow us to fight them on even terms for the control of the tachyonic particles they unleashed. We still have to find them and figure out how to fight them in battle, given they are so powerful. I'd do it at Ops' headquarters. Everyone can get there relatively quickly, and it's secure."

Medina nodded. "Agreed. This will certainly be a different type of company meeting."

Chapter Eleven
The Act
July 7, 2021

In 1974, Special Operations headquarters in Las Vegas was started. Since then, it had grown into a huge complex like a college campus. It was the foremost trauma recovery center in the country, because TMs tended to leave behind badly damaged victims. The campus had temporary and permanent housing and trauma recovery facilities, but also a large building that housed the government operation.

Given that Ops was in Vegas and it was July 7, it was unsurprisingly hot already despite being only 8:10 in the morning. The sun was bright, the cloud skyless, as befits the desert. The temperature was eighty-six degrees and felt much hotter in the sun.

Fortunately, Ops would be operating inside. Besides the government buildings and trauma hospital and treatment wings, there were many other facilities, including gyms, a baseball field Sam Grant had constructed when he was in charge, tennis courts, and soccer fields. There was also a huge dance floor with mirror showing in three directions. That's where the Ops team was gathering for the sex channeling effort.

Osa arrived first. She wore a black leotard with a light blue skirt over it and dance shoes. Entering, she looked around. The room was quiet. There were several metal folding chairs scattered about at random, but then four very specific wooden chairs set in what was clearly a square.

"Hello?"

"Come in! Hold on, I'm in back."

A moment later, Medina appeared. She was wearing a pink blouse and blue skirt with dance shoes. She approached and said, "Sorry, I'm doing some last-minute paperwork. The rest of us will be out in a bit."

"Got it."

Osa thought Medina seemed very nervous. She didn't know if that was good or bad, but her initial thought was it was bad. Then again, Osa was a bit nervous herself. But she was more intrigued. She liked discovering new things and wasn't at all self-conscious about this type of . . . assignment.

"Hi, this the right room?"

Osa turned to see Nicole. She wore navy blue leggings, a black sports bra, and a jeans jacket over that.

"Yep! Nice to meet you, Miss Carerra. I loved your newscasts on INN," said Nicole, almost gushing. "And I gotta say, I love your hair!"

"Thanks! I've got to see one of your plays," said Osa.

Nicole rolled her eyes as they shook hands.

Ashley arrived. She wore a yellow blouse and jeans. "Hi, ladies."

"Hi," they both said, and they all hugged.

Nicole said, "That is great perfume."

Ashley smiled. "I'll text you what I use. It's homemade."

"Get real!" said Osa, laughing.

"Is it just us? Where's the boss?" asked Ashley.

At that moment, Medina returned and clapped her hands. "Okay, ladies, we can chat like old gals at a church bingo later! Let's outline the plan."

"Do we get naked now?" asked Nicole. The others laughed.

Medina wagged a finger. "Don't get yourself in trouble, Miss Smith."

Nicole made a gesture of zipping her lips.

"Sam will explain the rest," she said.

From the side room, three men entered. Sam wore jeans and a purple Milwaukee Brewers T-shirt. Tripper entered wearing his typical getup of Atlanta Braves cap, old T-shirt, and jeans. The Radar robot stationed in Las Vegas was also there, Radar's consciousness in it. He wore a black T-shirt with a logo "Free Willie Nelson" over jeans and ratty sneakers.

Sam smiled. "Looking good, ladies."

"Hey, if we're going to be pervs, we want to look the part," said Nicole with a laugh. The other girls smiled.

Sam smiled.

Medina looked at them. "This is awkward, I know, but this is also very serious, ladies We're playing with a new type of channeling here, and embarrassment or hesitation can get us all killed, so it has to be serious."

"We know," said Ashley with a nod.

Radar turned to Tripper. "Our resident old fuck and me have done a lot of research on this, and we believe we can counter what the Quartet and friends did down in Teira del Fuego. You wanna explain, O'Sullivan?"

Tripper rose and leaned on his cane. "Yup, reckon I can. Okay, sex channeling is basically a form of geometric channeling that enhances the aural output through sexual acts. The strongest ones are anal, 'cause that can be performed by men and women."

Nicole looked around. "It's just us girls getting intimate, seems to me."

"Well, can don't mean is. We had no men volunteers, though I am manning the center, which is the key position with this spell."

Osa cocked her head. "So, we're the sacrifices buying you time and power by sitting around with our butts stuffed while the powerful man uses all his power? Who devised this ritual?"

"Ancient old men," said Tripper, "but like I said, it can be anyone in any spot. We just worked out that way 'cause all our boys are shy."

"Or old," added Sam.

"Or robots," added Radar.

"All the women in our organization are the ones that kick-ass channel," said Medina.

Tripper looked at her. "Y'all might well be more annoying than your big sis, and that's saying something."

Medina winked at him. "Continue your enthralling explanation."

"Anyhow, reckon like I was saying, our objective is to focus a direct counter-spell to the Consortium's efforts. We can't stop 'em from trying again, but we can annul their efforts down south."

"Does anyone know exactly what they did?" asked Ashley. "I mean, I'm the last person to apologize for those assholes. They threw me in Mars prison for months and killed one of my friends in the battle on Storm Island. But maybe whatever they did isn't that dangerous? What is this particle? The QPC — a quantum probability cloud particle, you called it in the write-up."

Osa quickly said, "And why dig up an ancient art no one knows about for something minor?"

"She's right," said Sam. "We don't know what it does, Ashley, but it's permeating the globe. Our spell can counter it. It can stop it from saturating the globe, which hopefully will stop their plan or maybe give us a clue as to what it does. Unfortunately, they killed our main resource, Doctor Tang, so we're operating purely on theory and common sense."

Ashely nodded. "I agree, if we can't determine if it's hostile, we assume it to be as such."

"If everyone is agreed for this, then I suggest we prepare and start. This will not be an easy spell. Tripper has to manipulate a lot of energy and it will take probably ten to twelve minutes."

"Who, that's a long time," said Nicole.

"I know, youngin', but it's a tricky spell."

"Sam, we'll get prepared in here. You three go to the auxiliary room."

"Right. C'mon, old fuck," said Sam.

Tripper chuckled. "Reckon I still walk better than your arthritic ass."

Radar said nothing, unusually sullen, still chafing over his failure to stop the ritual two weeks earlier. He knew if anyone was hurt, it was his failure that was the cause.

Once the men exited, Medina took the lead. "You've heard what we've got to do. This will be really difficult."

Ashley immediately sat on the arm of the couch and said, "So was stopping Calico and the Consortium. But we did it. And we'll do this. We can't allow this to happen. This group of Consortium leaders is no different than Calico. They're murdering thousands, millions to get what can be achieved by other means."

"I agree," said Nicole, sitting on the soft to Ashley's right.

Osa was standing and sat on the other side of the sectional as she said, "Medina, we are united. We want to do this. So, let's get to it."

Medina nodded. "Okay. But this will be hard physically and emotionally. We must be strong, united."

"We don't need a pep talk," said Nicole. "We will do this." Then she frowned. "Although you're right about the physical part. Sliding up and down that thing for upwards of ten minutes is a lot harder than it looks."

"Yeah, it's worse than gym class with your period," said Ashley.

Medina smiled. "Yeah. Okay, I did talk with Tripper. We don't have to be nude. I suggest we all wear something like a nightgown so we're not nude."

"I'm for that," said Osa.

"I'll get them from the supply room," said Medina. Ops' Vegas facility was one of the foremost in the world for trauma recovery, and as a result had a number of permanent guests. They routinely had clothes on hand. "I'm ordering us all black."

"Works for us," said Osa, and the others nodded.

"Okay. Let's check out the chairs."

She led them to the square. The chairs were wooden with light varnish. The centers had a strange metal circle in them, which the girls correctly assumed was where the dildo would be held.

Nicole said, "Medina, none of ever asked exactly how much is going to the back door."

"Five inches. It's an inch for each member of the spell."

"Average then," said Nicole, hands on her hips. Then she looked at Ashley. "Uh, not to be all invasion of privacy stalker, but have you two done this? I mean, I tried a couple times and it's not my thing, but I've done it."

"I was a servant in the Society and then a double-agent in the Consortium. You can pretty much figure if it exists, I tried it," said Osa, rolling her eyes.

"I'm like you, a little college experimentation. I can handle it," said Ashley.

"Now that we're past that," said Medina quickly, "we can talk details."

"What about you, boss?"

Medina shot her a look to kill and said, "Information regarding that is confidential."

The women all laughed. Ashley then said, "Now we'll *never* rest until we know the secret."

Medina blushed and said, "If we survive this, fine. Because there's danger here, okay?' She was eager to change the subject. The girls fell into line. "The psychic heat feedback could be critical. The Consortium group in Tiera de Fuego had snow around them, but we think that coincidence. However, we picked this room as it's open space, reinforced against fire so we don't burn the place down, and we're above the swimming pool, just as a precaution."

"Sensible," said Osa.

Nicole studied the chair. "So, we sit and slide while Tripper does all the real work."

"Basically, yeah," said Medina.

Nicole shrugged. "Well, let's get to it."

At that moment, the runner with the nightgowns arrived.

The girls changed. They weren't modest, they were professionals, and they were eager to start. But as they changed, Ashley looked worried and said, "There's one issue to consider. The psychic heat. What if we get backflow and *can't* cool it?"

"Then we're dead," said Medina.

Ashley shook her head. "No, I know that. I mean, I have confidence we and Tripper can manage it, but it could get hot . . . under us."

Now Osa widened her eyes. "Oh, shit."

"Ah, I get it," said Medina.

Nicole said, "I'm with them, boss. I can handle it if it's, uh, sore from the, ah, duration. But I don't want my ass literally cooked."

"We've got hoses ready," said Medina.

"Okay, good. I should've known you'd be prepared," said Ashley with a smile, buttoning up.

"Thanks," said Medina.

The women were ready, wearing nightgowns without underwear. The gowns were all the same, simple long, black night gowns that were loose fitting.

Nicole laughed. "Y'know, doing weird shit like this is probably why we're all single."

"Uh, well . . . confession time, darlings, I've had a second date with a guy named Ken Hurst I knew in college briefly," said Ashley.

"You wench! You have a man and haven't told us!" shouted Medina, pointing accusingly.

Ashley smiled. "Hey, I've been busy! And it may go nowhere. He's really into having kids, which, you know, can be tricky for us."

The women all nodded. Channelers generally had a hard time getting pregnant, because it altered their aura. It certainly wasn't an absolute. Geraldine Kane, for example, had birthed both Medina and Geneva. But it was a concern . . . aside from the normal concerns of being in such a dangerous profession.

"Still, we'll see. If we survive *this* debacle," she said dryly.

"Uh, let's talk logistics. What exactly are we riding?" asked Osa.

Medina held up a finger. "Hold on." Then she went to the other room, then returned with a small black box.

"Do we get to pick colors?" asked Nicole.

"They're all the same. This is for work, not play," teased Medina.

Inside the box were four identical vibrators that had very smooth surfaces and were able to be bolted into the chairs.

"Not cosmetically appealing, but I guess it will do the job," said Osa.

"My thoughts exactly," said Nicole with a smile.

"Let's get them set up."

"Uh, you have good lube, right? Because that's really the secret to this," said Osa.

"I have the best."

Nicole took the first one. "What the Hell, let's get this done."

"Yeah," said Osa.

"I'm ready," said Ashley, clearly more nervous.

"And I get the last one. Ah, well."

The girls moved to the chairs and locked their dildos into position.

Ashley positioned herself over the chair and said, "Jesus, I feel like I'm getting potty trained."

They all laughed, must more than the joke justified, all nervous. They were all a little embarrassed, but also knew this was a very serious spell and they could well end the night injured or dead.

Osa didn't waste any time. Once her dildo was locked, she lubed it, lubed her butt, and lowered herself cautiously. Then she shrugged. "Nice fit."

Medina laughed. "You say that now. Say that fifteen minutes from now."

Nicole lowered, as did Medina. Ashley went the slowest. She had some trouble, but she made it.

Medina clapped. "Come on, guys, we're on the clock."

Tripper entered. He and Sam had been going over all the measurements, the precautions, the emergency plan, as if they were emergency workers preparing for a plane headed for the airport without rudder control. Radar was staying back as last-ditch fire prevention if it all went south, as flame couldn't hurt him.

Moving quickly to the middle, Tripper nodded at Medina and said, "Ladies, I'm ready. Reckon I appreciate all y'alls help an' I hope I don't fuck it up."

"You'll do fine. Ready, ladies?" asked Medina.

They nodded. Sam said, "I've got the clock and EMT services. Go for it."

Tripper put his cane down in the exact center and began to channel, while simultaneously the women began to slowly ride up and down on their dildo chairs.

Immediately, Tripper began to perspire. He had a purple and yellow glow around him.

"What's that?" asked Ashley.

"Probability cloud influence," said Medina, surprised. "Hold tight. Don't stop!"

Ashley grunted. The women began to perspire as well, as it began to heat up in the room.

Osa said worriedly, "Medina, it's already getting hot!"

"Hold on!"

Sam snapped, "It's just the exertion! You're okay. The temperature is normal! The psychic heat register is well below danger range!"

"We got it, Sam," said Nicole.

Ashley looked very worried. Nicole kept concentrating. Osa was flushed and looed panicked, and Medina looked concerned but determined. None of them stopped.

Tripper spun his cane around like a magician's wand and the purple and gold trail followed it. "Darn shit messin' up the balance."

"Stop showing off and get this over with," muttered Osa.

"We're barely into this!" shouted Medina. "It's three minutes."

"Oh, fuck me, and I am not making a joke!" whined Nicole.

"Ride it or die!" snapped Medina.

"I'm riding!" shouted Nicole.

Tripper, however, was struggling in a way he didn't expect. "Probability surge . . . reckon the Consortium . . . they might've known we'd track down . . . this shit."

"What's that mean?" shouted Sam, growing alarmed.

"Almost like spell is . . . working again' me. Like swimming upstream . . . shouldn't be like that," he muttered, and he tossed off his baseball cap to reveal a drenched forehead and sweaty hair stuck to his head.

The women kept moving up and down, trying to focus on their job. Sam crossed his fingers unconsciously. He was alarmed. If Tripper lost control, they would almost certainly all die. At the very least, they'd be violently expelled from the geometric form, in this case the square composed by the chairs, and given they were, ah, impaled . . . they could be gravely injured.

"The spell is . . . alive?" asked Medina.

"Hard to explain."

"I've never heard of anything like that, not even from my sister," said Medina.

"Reckon it's rare. Not alive . . . sentient," he said, grunting. Now he held his cane over his head and started spinning it, creating a kaleidoscope of purple and yellow across the room. "It's only 'cause it's probability tachyonic matrix at work here. At first, it resisted me. Quantum physics. Observing it activated it. But now I got the swing of it."

"Luckily for you, so do we," said Nicole sarcastically.

Ashley was still focused, and she was very flushed. She felt a lot of pain at first, but she had adjusted to the tempo and suddenly realized shew as on the verge of an orgasm. She absolutely couldn't believe it.

"Sam, y'all should evacuate," said Tripper.

"No way!"

"We're only seven minutes in. Ain't sure I'm a'gonna hold it. If there's a tachyonic implosion and a psychic heat release, there ain't no point in y'all goin' down with the ship."

"I can help," said Sam, though he really couldn't.

"Out, Grant. That's an order!" shouted Medina.

Sam looked at her. "It's really hard to take you seriously when you're sitting there with something rammed up your butt while you try to boss me around."

"Out!"

He reluctantly obeyed, but he didn't go far. He just went outside the dance studio, which had a window from which he could observe. He called Radar, "Be ready."

"I am. But I can't move fast enough to save 'em all, Sam. If it goes, some will die."

Nicole grunted. "Jesus, my legs are killing me. No one said this was like doing eight minutes worth of squats!"

Tripper snapped, "Ah, shuddup! A porn star can do a twenty-minute scene without complaining!"

"That, I am quite certain, is not true," said Osa.

"Wait . . . holy smokes! Hold on, ladies!" said Tripper with suddenness and wide eyes.

Before anyone could react, a purple and yellow cone suddenly dropped over him, as if someone had taken a tornado, painted it, and dropped it on him like a cone.

"Ahhhhhhhhhhhhhh!" shouted Nicole.

"God, what is that?" shrieked Osa.

"*Don't stop ramming!*" shouted Medina, panicking, afraid if they stopped now it would be fatal to all of them.

Ashley said nothing, her orgasm having ceased, and now she just felt . . . full. And scared.

Tripper put up his hands and suddenly he was moving inside what looked like a suite of yellow and purple cones.

And he was talking.

"Who're y'all?" he snapped.

The man smiled and rose. "Doxom James."

Tripper stared. They were standing on a rocky hill, and behind Tripper were screams and the smell of sulfur. For a moment, he almost panicked and thought he was in Hell, but the sky was normal. The sky in Hell was red . . . though most of the memories of Hell faded, that was one that remained.

Doxom was a tall man with receding black hair streaked with gray that was straight, short, and parted to the right. He had a thick but short mustache that covered just his upper lip. His jaw was jutting and his blue eyes piecing. He moved aggressively and spoke quickly as he rose from the rock. He wore a blue suit with a red and white striped tie.

"O'Sullivan, do you know where we are?"

"Not a clue."

"You're reaching me through psychic energy. That's what sex channeling opens up. You know who I am?"

"Not a clue. Uh, exceptin' y'all gave me your name of Dox Ham."

"Dox-om! Look, I can explain. You need to shut down the spell and come to me. I'm from Atlantia."

Tripper, of course, knew of the ancient undersea kingdom that had once been a city in Egypt. Marrina and the Mind of the Gods moved it to a secure location under the Arctic sea thousands of years ago, but in 2020 the Gods had abandoned Earth and taken Atlantia with them to a different dimensional plane.[18]

"Do tell."

"This is all part of a safety plan. How fast can you get to Seattle?"

"Reckon a few hours. We're in Vegas."

"Good. Drag your hillbilly ass to Mercer Island. Then follow the probability trail. Fast."

"Ya got it."

Then he was gone.

Suddenly, the purple and yellow cone vanished, and Tripper was standing, staring absently over Medina's head.

"He's normal again!" shouted Osa.

"We can see that," snapped Medina.

Tripper shook his head. "Holy shit, this ain't what I expected, but I think it worked. Let me ramp down the spell."

He did that, which took only seconds, then said, "We're good, we're done. You can stop."

---

[18] See TM 3.1 "Escape"

The women all gasped a huge sigh of relief and, exhausted, they simply sat on their dildo chairs for several seconds. All were soaked in perspiration and red from exertion.

Sam quickly entered the room. "That was 9:29. What did you learn?"

"Uh, a minute, guys. Fuck. This was hard," said Nicole.

"Yeah, my shoulders are shot," said Medina. "I was pushing myself with my shoulders because my legs gave out long ago. I gotta get more time in the gym."

Osa smiled. "Well, I guess I'm the slut of the group, because I did just fine. But I would like this thing out of my ass."

Sam said, "Tripper and I will talk in the office. Radar is going to your office, Medina, to get readings on the spell."

Medina nodded and looked at Ashley, who was just sitting and looked a little bewildered. "Ash, you okay, babe?"

"Uh, I'm fine," she said, looking down.

Medina didn't push it. She looked at Osa, then at Nicole. "Thank God we're in Ops and not porn. Okay, the boys are in the other room. Let's lift off."

The women all rose. Nicole groaned and stretched her back once she was up, and Medina rubbed her hamstrings.

"My ass will be sore for a month," bitched Nicole.

"Probably longer," said Osa with a wink.

Nicole said, "Bite me, Carrera."

Osa laughed.

Medina groaned as she rose and said, "I'm with Nicole. I may never crap right again."

That broke the tension and made them all laugh.

But Ashley laughed nervously.

"What're they laughing about?" asked Tripper, wiping off his forehead with a paper towel.

"Probably made a joke. They're all nervous. What did you see?"

"Just a guy, but he's important."

"So, you didn't stop what the Consortium did?"

"No. All I got was a name and a location for some help. Basically, whole thing amounted to nothing more than a long-distance phone call. Put out the dog and piss on the fire, Sam. We're a'headin' to Seattle."

Chapter Twelve
Doxom James
July 7, 2021

"Nice digs," said Sam as they met Doxom James at his multi-million-dollar home on Mercer Island.

"It's a place," said Doxom, shaking Sam's hand. He wore a gray suit with an expensive watch, new black tie, and was clearly wearing hair gel.

Sam and Tripper looked a bit dowdy compared to him. Tripper wore his usual outfit, though he'd put on a clean T-shirt. Sam wore jeans, a black and red checkered shirt, and a jeans jacket. They were both tired.

After a quick meeting with Medina, the two men had immediately worked with the NSA to get a military flight out of Vegas to Seattle, then been driven by an NSA agent to Doxom's home on Mercer Island. Radar and the others stayed behind to start preparations, and also just in case it was all a waste of time or a trap, though Radar was listening via com-link.

Besides, Medina thought the women needed a break. The channeling effort had been psychologically and physically exhausting for them, and they wanted to be ready for action if the men came back with news. Tripper, ironically, wound up with the easy job in the spell when it seemed on the surface he would have the hardest.

The Vegas to Seattle trip took about four hours, so it was around two in the afternoon when they arrived. And it was gorgeous, eighty-four degrees and sunny with a few light clouds.

"Let's go out by the rose garden," said Doxom. "I've won awards."

"Reckon they's worth seein', then," said Tripper.

They followed him down a freshly mown lawn to a beautiful rose garden, some of which were in a greenhouse, some of which were planted outdoors, and some of which were in moveable transport and currently sitting outdoors getting some sun. There were all types and all colors.

"Smells like a woman's perfume store. You must be proud," said Sam.

"I am." Then Doxom said quickly and serious, "But I'm scared. It's a good thing you got hold of me. Time is quickly running out."

"Always is in these things, I reckon," said Tripper, leaning on his right side on his cane.

Doxom offered a seat on a wooden bench near some white roses. Sam sat, but Tripper declined and said, "I'd rather stand. Planes and me don't get along too well."

Doxom said on a bench cross a stone path from Sam. There were no weeds. He said, "Your choice. I suggest we get to business. We have to make plans."

"Sure. So, who are you and what do you know about this giant cock-up?" asked Sam.

"As I told Tripper during the spell when our minds linked, I'm Doxom James and originally from Atlantia," he said.

"Why are you here now?" asked Sam. "I thought the Gods abandoned Earth."[19]

"Good question," said Doxom with a smile. "When the Gods left, they had concerns about problems on Earth eventually propagating to the destruction of the planet. They didn't leave on a whim, boys. They left because they knew if Quotient discovered them, it would

---

[19] See TM 3.1 "Escape"

alter his perceptions immeasurably and they knew, he-it being a toddler, that it would be a lethal combination."

"Dunno. Our version is that they turned tail and ran," said Tripper, clearly putting his own feelings on the actual version of events. In truth, Ops knew little of the Gods retreat. They had slain Heidi Minor, their new Marrina, and allowed Donovan to return her body to Ops and announce they were leaving.

Then they were gone, and they hadn't come back despite Quotient being dispatched . . . at least, to Ops' minds. The true story was much more complex.

Doxom shook his head. "No. They left to ensure that they weren't the cause of humanity's destruction."

"But they haven't returned," said Sam pointedly.

"Because the danger *isn't* over. They left me and some others who . . . specialize . . . in certain lost but dangerous arts. Sex channeling is one of them. You see, I was originally a resident of Sodom."

"Was it as bad as Vegas?" asked Tripper.

Doxom snorted. "Sodom was a shithole. It was a land of survival of the fittest and it deserved its fate." He paused. "I don't know how you found out about sex channeling, but it is a very complicated art."

"We learned from this woman down in Texas who can communicate with the dead."

Doxom nodded. "The dead know. The dead know everything." He looked serious and agitated, always fidgeting, always moving, and perspiring heavily even though, while warm, it wasn't a particularly hot day. Bees buzzed him, drawn by the roses and perspiration.

"Reckon so. So, what all does this do, besides give cult leaders another way to trick dumb or desperate girls into droppin' their skirts?" asked Tripper.

"Sex channeling can be used to perform radical, probability altering events. If done properly, the probability cone it can create makes a probability cloud look like drizzle compared to a thunderstorm." He paused. "Understand, some of us . . . we knew this in Sodom. And we were scared. We prayed, and the Mind of the Gods answered. They helped us destroy Sodom and Gammorah, not God. Unless, of course, you consider that God sent us the Mind of the Gods."

"Always a possibility," said Sam diplomatically.

Doxom frowned and nodded, biting his lip. "Regardless, they gassed the place. I don't know the details. It wasn't pretty. That's when I became a citizen of Atlantia, to my great pride." He blew out some air. "But it's not an easy job, and now we have a mess."

"Mess?" asked Sam.

"I read what you sent me," said Doxom after biting his right thumbnail. "Your friend Radar was right, the spell is a primer. The spell in South America released probability cloud, PC, particles into the air. They are unique. Every PC particle released by sex channeling is unique because they are quantum PC particles."

"So, the user, presumably the casters, alter the particles simply by observing them, by knowing they are there," said Sam thoughtfully.

"Yes."

"That's damn silly," said Tripper.

Doxom looked at him with chagrin. "That's quantum physics, hillbilly! Look, that's not important. The key is they work together like a net and bestow incredible probability altering power on the users."

"But surely if it's a primer, we have time to stop it," said Sam.

Tripper nodded.

Doxom shook his head. "You do and you don't. There's a kicker to this spell, a real barbed hook. Stopping these idiots before the spell starts won't stop the spell. It will still leave the lethal PC force in the air for anyone to jump up and control. The only way to permanently end it is to disrupt the spell *once the channeling starts*. There's about a twenty-minute window. So, this is one risky son of a bitch."

"Damn," said Sam, which pretty much said it all.

Tripper frowned. "Y'all know a lot. Y'all had to have a sense this was goin' on. Why're you helping us now?"

"Alone, I can't possibly beat them. I got a sense of the spell, and I've been working backwards ever since. In another few days, I would have contacted you if you had not reached me. I don't see any way to pull this off without a concentrated effort *after* they start."

"I agree, we can't leave this shit floating around in the atmosphere, but this is a huge risk. What if we miss the window?" asked Sam.

"Then they win, and they'll do whatever they're going to do."

"Reckon we don't know what that is entirely, but we think they wanna push earth into a," and he made air quotes, "Golden Age and get ridda all electronic activity."

Doxom whistled. "Boy, that will kill a lot of people."

"They think it will stop global warming, which it will. Of course, as usual, the Consortium cares little for collateral damage," said Sam with disgust. "Billions will die with the power to farm, to heat, and so on. They know this. They just don't care."

Tripper said, "What if we just whup-ass on them so they can't run the spell?"

"Well, the problem is, if you just go arrest them or throw the off a building or whatever you people do, the spell is still armed. Someone might figure out a much worse use for it," said Doxom.

"Or it might just fade away," said Sam.

Doxom immediately shook his head. "It doesn't work that way." Then he chuckled darkly. "It would be damn nice if it did. But it will be sitting around like a nuclear bomb waiting for activation."

"Okay. We had a reading that it would take up to 32 days to saturate the earth. When would they do the next spell?"

"Theoretically, at any point after that," said Doxom.

"That ain't no answer," muttered Tripper.

"Well, it is," said Sam, rubbing his chin. "They would be unlikely to wait long. Someone could steal their particles, and they also risk getting caught beforehand."

Doxom looked at Tripper and pointed at Sam. "I'm with him."

Tripper chuckled. "Me, too, I reckon. Right. What's our next move?"

Sam said with a cold face, "We find these goat fuckers and make sure this time they're the ones taking it up the ass."

Radar said, "Doxom, can we predict when they'll do the spell?"

"I can get you a two-hour window, but only if we know where the spell is going to be executed from."

Tripper sighed. "Always gotta be a complication."

"Not a bad one this time," said Radar, suddenly interrupting via the com-link. "I've researched. To run the spell, they need to sacrifice auras, and a lot of them. It's kind of like Quotient used to feed on souls, like he did in Portland. But this one has to be very isolated as it's long. People can't run away. So, there's logically only one place they can run it. That would be Valeria's castle in the capitol of Glickstenstein, which has a prison with 1,500 or so political prisoners underneath it."

"I'd go with that," said Sam.

"Damn straight," agreed Tripper.

"Very well. Give me a moment." Doxom pulled out his phone and said, "Local time, that is time at the location, maximum potential is two to four in the afternoon on July 8."

"Shit! That's two days," said Tripper, ripping off his baseball cap, wiping his hair, and putting it back on.

"Less than that," said Sam. "They're nine hours ahead over there."

"I'm glad to come with and assist. Just let me get a backpack," said Doxom, turning to enter the house.

Sam grabbed him gently and said, "No, Doxom. We need you out of this in case we fail. You're the only one that knows shit about this and could organize a second attempt to stop them."

Doxom looked heartbroken. "I . . . don't know what to say." He paused, nodded to himself, and said, "But I will respect your wishes."

Sam turned to Radar. "We have to get to Europe and quick. Check with Medina on who's available." Sam turned to Tripper. "How is Geneva?"

"Still fussin' with figuring out her whole power thing from that battle with Calico and fightin' in Eruope." Back in December, Geneva had undergone a tachyon influx from Calico in an attack, which allowed her to transmute objects. But that was temporary, and her powers and fatigue level had been shifting wildly in the months since.

"Then she stays out. She, Doxom, and Little Jack can coordinate second efforts. I'm not sure how Geneva, Little Jack or his sisters would react to the tachyonic surge that's going to happen in that castle."

Radar said quickly, "I'm with you there. So, we probably have my European robot, keeping the others in reserve, you, Searly, Medina, Osa, Ashley, and Thunder. We might be able to get Nicole. Her power would help. Anyone's will help."

"We'll make it work. Let's get back to Vegas. We've got a lot to do. We might as well call Medina and have her break the news to the ladies that the party is over."

Chapter Thirteen
Ashley and Osa Talk Sex

After Medina had finished her quick meeting with Tripper and Sam before their flight, she had returned to the main room where the women were nervously moving the chairs.

"Let's clean up, ladies. I have to stay on duty, but I think you three need to rest. If Tripper and Sam get some info, we may have to move fast."

"I just want to sleep. Can I have a guest room here or something?" asked Nicole.

"Yeah, just check at the front desk."

"Thanks." She turned. "It was fun, ladies, but I want a douche, a shower, and a nap."

"Thanks for your help, Nicole," said Osa.

"Yeah, you're a trooper," said Ashley.

She smiled, winked, and sauntered off, clearly exhausted.

Medina asked, "You two?"

"I just want a shower and I'll be back. I want to study what Radar learned and hear what Tripper discovered," said Ashley.

"I feel the same," said Osa. She turned to Ashley, "We can shower in the locker room, grab some candy, and come back?"

Nervously, Ashley said, "Uh, sure. Sure."

"Okay. I don't have time for a shower, which sure isn't all that comfortable with all this goop in my butt, but that's the price of being a leader," grumbled Medina. "But you can bring me back a Hershey's bar. With almonds. Or you're fired."

"On it, boss," said Osa with a smile.

Osa and Ashley exited the room and walked to the showers, which were just down the hall, as Osa said, "I'm very tired as well. It was quite an exercise."

"Not one . . . I mean, not what I expected," said Ashley nervously.

The women's locker room was small and square, with benches along three sides and an open wall on the far side with five showers. The room was exceptionally clean with white tile and an aqua-marine colored floor. Two benches ran parallel near the lockers on the sides. Near the door was a new trash bin.

Once they reached the locker room, Ashley suddenly said, "I might just go lay down."

Osa took Ashley's purse, put it in a locker, and said, "My friend, obviously something during this happened that has upset you."

"Ah, I'm just tired," said Ashley, clearly trying to dodge the issue.

Osa put her hands on her hips and said, "Ashley, I don't know you very well at all, but I *do* know an upset woman. You can't hide from your feelings. It's best to talk about them, and given Nicole can be a little abrasive and Medina is your boss, you probably have to talk to me — or talk to a stuffed animal."

Ashely smiled. "You have a unique way of putting things. Where are you from?"

She smiled. "New Mexico."

Ashely flushed. "It's hard to talk about . . . it's . . . hard."

Osa cocked her head. "I don't think so. Only two things could upset you this much. Either you had some manner of flashback to prior trauma . . . or you had an orgasm. And not knowing your background, I don't know which, but I do know neither is anything to be ashamed of or embarrassed about. Both are natural reactions."

Looking shocked, Ashley flushed beet red. She sat on the bench, Osa sitting to her right side as Ashley stammered, "I . . . I . . . oh."

Osa smiled gently and put a hand on Ashley's right shoulder. "Orgasm. It's *okay*. It's the body's way of protecting itself."

Ashley was beet red and distraught as she said in a soft, pained voice, "I just . . . can't believe *under those circumstances* I could . . . do that."

Seeing how shaken Ashley was, Osa gently said, "Dear, it's okay. Some women orgasm during rape. It's the body's physical reaction and a form of protection. It doesn't mean they enjoyed it."

"I have always felt in control . . . I'm just . . . I didn't think I was like that."

"Like what? Human? A woman?"

"Just . . . primitive. I feel . . . like a slut."

Osa was concerned. "These are value judgements you are placing on a physical reaction to stress. That's all. This isn't about how you felt. It's about how you're making yourself feel now."

Ashley looked at her. "I'm ashamed. That's all there is to it."

"I can understand your feelings. I can empathize. But you're too good of a woman to do this to yourself."

Ashley looked a little angry now, angry at herself. "How could I get pleasure when I'm trying to save the world and trying to . . . I'm in control. I shouldn't be able to go there unless I *want* to. I'm not that way."

"Ah . . . I see," said Osa gently. Osa then cocked her head and said, "Who you are is not always the same. Who you are is based on circumstances."

"To a degree. Not for stuff like this."

Osa nodded. "I will share with you, because it may help. Have you read my file?"

Ashley narrowed her eyes. "Yes, but I assume there's more to it."

"Of course. My family was Society, and I came to Ops for protection. I believed in the Society. But to fully appreciate the Society, I was a servant there for nearly a year."

Ashley arched an eyebrow. "That isn't in the file."

"I prefer it to not be generally known. I am not ashamed of it, but people's value judgements might affect how they react. I learned many things as a servant. I learned the value of freedom, first and foremost. But I also learned sex is a biological function. I did many things with many different types of people." She smiled. "I never saw myself as a slut. That's a value judgement. I was doing a job, which sometimes was enjoyable and sometimes was not. But my body always responded. It's supposed to do that. It's how we're protected. Your shame is purely your own doing."

Ashley took a deep breath. "I . . . Osa, I'm not a prude, but I'm a pretty straightforward girl from Washington. I never was kinky, and all my sex is pretty much straight sex and oral with men I cared about. I like emotional connection with sex. Sex for sex's sake is . . . meaningless. This was meaningless, yet my body acted as if it wasn't."

"Again, for protection," said Osa, holding up a finger, "And this was not meaningless. This was an attempt to help us save the world. I can think of nothing that has more meaning than that!"

Ashley was struck by this. She eventually nodded, smiled, and said, "You have a point there. You're very persuasive. No wonder you were so good reporting on TV."

Osa smiled politely. "I appreciate the compliment." She stood. "Come to my condo and shower there where you have privacy. We're on the campus if the others need us, and I can make some drinks while you clean up."

Ashley considered for a heartbeat, then said, "Okay. But this is just friends, okay? I'm not into girls."

Osa held up her hand. "I am a friend, nothing more. Nothing less, though."

"Okay. But I'm also gonna need ice cream."

"Sorry it's a bit of a mess," said Osa.

Ashley didn't know how to answer, because to her the place was immaculate. The Ops condos were expensive and well-built. Osa's place was very current, with stainless steel appliances in a large kitchen, and white upper and black lower counters under a countertop that was white with flecks of volcanic rock. The island was bigger than average, and spotless other than a knife rack. The table was black and small, but cute. There was a vase with red roses sitting in the middle. The only item the slightest bit out of place was an empty cookie jar on the dining room table.

The living area had a gray sofa, white bookcases along two walls, and the back wall was an open bar with barstools. Just past that was a bar with a decent selection of wines and booze. Although the door was shut, Ashley assumed the bathroom and bedroom were in the back, past the kitchen. The walls were covered with paints of leopards, cheetahs, and bobcats. And running around was a huge orange tabby that made Garfield look slim, Mister FattyPants.

"It's . . . pretty cool," said Ashley. "Hi, kitty."

Mister FattyPants ran away.

"Hah! Sorry, he's the picture of the scaredy cat," said Osa.

"You have a robe I can borrow?" asked Ashley.

"Yes, hanging on the back of the door. It's pink. I'll mix the drinks while you clean up."

"You don't want to clean up?" asked Ashley.

Osa laughed. "Trust me, I've spent many nights with a greased-up bottom. I do want to clean up, but I want some drinks a *lot* more."

Ashley smiled. "I'll be quick."

Osa mixed them drinks, humming the theme to a song she'd heard in the store a couple days ago, some sort of old Billy Idol tune. She made margaritas.

Ashely took only six minutes. She smiled and said, "You have a great hair dryer."

Osa fixed her with a stern look. "I went through six stores and eight orders to find that. If you broke it, you're dead."

Ashley laughed. "It's fine, but I guess knowing that, I won't bother to ask where you got it! This is a nice place."

Osa laughed and said, "I do like this place. It suits my life now. I miss home in New Mexico, but it's not far to visit mom and dad."

"You don't feel safe there?" asked Ashley, sipping her white drink and adding, "Oh, and this is good."

"Thanks," said Osa with a smile. "No, I'm afraid not. I have too many enemies." She paused. "As I mentioned, my parents were part of the Society, and I was as well after I turned 21. For years, I supported them and worked at INN. I . . . I believed in them, in their efforts. And a lot of them, probably eighty percent, were good people just helping turn around lives. It was only the inner circle and some of the upper echelon members that were really into these . . . these paranormal things that destroyed lives."

"It's that way with a lot of organizations," said Ashley. "I've been hanging with my parents in Centralia a lot. Thunder and I, and some others, we've used it as our unofficial base from which to help the people of Portland."

In September of 2020, the alien quotient, under command of Consortium leader Calico Kelkirk, sucked the souls and lives of most of the Portland population, about two million people in all. Thunder, Searly, Ashley, and Tripper had been in Portland and barely escaped when Tripper got them underground.

"It's a good effort of you to do so," said Osa, handing Ashley a margarita.

"Nice. Salty." Ashley put the drink down on the bar and said, "We almost died there."

Osa arched an eyebrow. "What happened?"

Osa knew from reading Ops' files, but she wanted to hear it first-hand. Ashley told her, unaware she had tears in her eyes. She finished by saying, "The worst part was the *silence*. No screams. No traffic. No shouts. No machines. No birds. Just . . . dead air."

"Truly awful. And yet you are worried about an orgasm."

Startled, Ashley said, "Well, yes. But not as much anymore. I guess you're right. I need to keep perspective."

"I think you do that very well. You seem a fine woman with good values and love for your parents and co-workers."

Ashley flushed. "Perhaps. I had a traditional upbringing, but my parents are pretty liberal. I'm more conservative than they are!"

Osa sipped her drink and licked her lips. "Ah, I serve an excellent bar. Okay, now Thunder. Have you and he been to bed?"

"No," said Ashley with a weird face. "He's twice my age. Yuck."

Osa arched an eyebrow. "Not even on Mars prison?"

Ashley rolled her eyes and groaned. "God, no. God, I hated that place. It wasn't overtly abusive. But being kidnapped and isolated was horrible. I mean, we got new arrivals at times, so we had news. But when someone got zapped in from, you know, Moscow, they didn't have much American news for us. You start to feel like you're in a nursing home and get very . . . blah. They drugged us, too." She then looked scared. "But I'd take that over what we went through in Portland any day. I was sure my soul would be shattered. You cannot understand fear until that moment."

"I'm sorry."

"Anyhow, uh, no. No sex with Bogut," she said, eager to stop talking about Portland.

Osa smiled. "Well, I was just talking sex, not marrying him. Older men can be exceptionally passionate with a younger woman. One of the things I learned in the Society."

"Well, still no. It would be weird. He's like . . . it would be like doing one of my dad's friends. Nope."

"I see." She gestured and they sat on the sofa. "I have thought of him. He's quite attractive."

"Are you bisexual?"

"I think many women are bisexual to a degree. I prefer males for, ah, mating, however."

"Well, if you want Thunder, you can have him. All he does at my house is belch and fart."

They both laughed.

Ashley downed her margarita and said, "That was good. Can I have another?"

"Of course! There's no limit at Osa's bar."

And there wasn't. They each had three and were about to break into the ice cream when Medina called.

Ashley sighed. "Party's over."

"We'll have another when this is over" said Osa, then she answered her phone. "Hi, boss. I'm here with Ashley . . . ah, I see. We'll be right over."

Ashley arched an eyebrow. "Trouble?"

"Most likely. They want a meeting. They need to talk about Glickstenstein."

"Then I shall shower, and we shall dress and join Medina in her office. Grab her candy."

Ashley said, "Thanks for the talk. It really helped stabilize me."

"I'm a friend. Friends always keep the balance."

Chapter Fourteen
Morrison and Team
July 8, 2021

"Everything is set," said Morrison as he marked the last point in white paint, then sat down the paint can, roller, and his laser measuring tool.

"Good. Preparation is key," said Valeria.

They were in a conference room of a medieval castle that also served as a prison for Valeria's political prisoners and torture magic victims. The conference room was sterile and surprisingly like a break room in an insurance company: white circular tables, gray cabinets, marble counter stops, a white refrigerator, seating for about two dozen. The light was too bright and the tile gray and tacky.

Sixty-six-year-old David Morrison looked pedestrian, wearing a black and white plaid shirt, jeans, and sneakers. He was a slightly overweight, tall man with a big nose, tiny ears, and shortly cut blond-gray hair. His blue eyes looked alert. Overall, he wasn't ugly or handsome, he just sort of. . . was. But he was powerful, his normalcy hiding exceptional paranormal power. A former film producer, he was also quite wealthy. His interest in the paranormal jumped after he had a heart attack and in a near death experience (NDE) met his wife. That led to other NDE experiences where he met more of the dead.

Morrison sat down in a gray folding chair, one of several. Most of them were on a cart ready to roll forward at the appropriate time, but a couple were sitting around. He patted the chair next to him. "Sit for a minute, then we can join the others for supper. I'm tired."

"You have done a fine job. You have been working hard for days," she said imperiously.

Valeria seemed to say everything imperiously, as if she'd seen too many leftover 1950s movies about Nazis. She spoke with an Eastern European accent, something like Polish, which was fitting because the thirty-four-year-old Valeria von Strussman was ruler of Glickstenstein, the postage-stamp sized company wedged between Poland and Belarus. The country wasn't part of NATO nor part of the Russian block. They were small, but they were powerful. Valeria was also an incredibly powerful torture magician that had access to certain information most didn't.

She was also beautiful. She prided herself on her beauty. Her chin was a little too angular, but otherwise she was poster-perfect. Her eyes were sky-blue. Her hair was dark, long, and straight, and framed her face perfectly. Her bosom was larger than normal and rode high, her hips the perfect ratio, and her appearance impeccable. She did this without a glamour, which a TM could use to alter his or her appearance to look younger or older — the aura could affect DNA. To Valeria, a glamour was a mark of failure.

Valeria had engaged in a few of the snuff film productions of Blue Moon, Morgana and Sunset's current production company. After all, given they were both supposedly dead, killed by Nicole Smith in 2017,[20] they had to have some layers of protection. They did that by continually shifting the legal entities of the production companies around. Valeria was happier now. She preferred being in Glickstenstein where she had absolute control.

"I can't fail at this," said Morrison, surprisingly pensive. He leaned forward with his elbows on his knees and made a fist on which he rested his head.

"We will succeed, but obviously, you are concerned, which I understand. This is a large endeavor."

---

[20] See TM 4.1 "Killer Inside"

"I'm mostly worried about the new girls. I know Sunset and Morgana can pull their weight. But Tasha and Donna? I dunno. Tasha has a lot of power. She could rival me one day. But she's not the sharpest tool in the shed. Donna is in Morgana's class. I know they both believe in all of this, but it's one thing to believe and another to be fully committed."

"They are committed, David. Trust me on this," she said with an unusually gentle smile.

He smiled back. "You're almost always right."

"Almost?"

He laughed. "Well, no one's perfect." Then he frowned and looked around. "Hey, where are the new girls, anyhow? I haven't seen them in hours."

Valeria rolled her eyes. "They're playing with toys in guest master bedroom six."

"Toys?"

"Fuck my ass!" shouted Tasha, laying on her back on the bed with Donna standing at the edge of the bed.

"I'm planning to," said Donna Kushner.

Then she stared to slide the strap-on into Tasha's bottom.

Tasha moaned. Twenty-year-old Tasha Morgan was a tall, thin girl with chestnut brown hair that was straight on top and ended in curls that swung around her shoulders. She had a high forehead, an angular jaw, pretty brown eyes, and a bit of a crook in her nose. Collagen had given her a bit of a thicker lower bottom lip than was natural, but the look worked. She had a small light brown birthmark on her right cheek. Her look was pretty and Ukrainian. Her demeanor and posture was gentle and submissive. She had been a simple porn and snuff film actress until Sunset recruited her for the first part of the Golden Age plan. During that spell, Tasha manifested latent paranormal ability that was powerful, but that hadn't changed her yet. She was only a neophyte with the paranormal, having been involved for just a few weeks.

"Uhhhhhhhhh, yeah, oh, God," moaned Tasha as Donna went in slowly and deeply.

Donna smiled. She was twenty-six, a buxom brunette with long, straight hair and bangs. Her eyes were bright blue. She was very attractive. Now twenty-six, she had been in the Society since she was rescued from a cult in Iowa at age twenty, where they tried to sacrifice her in a torture magic ritual. After her normal servitude, she'd gotten into the sex entertainment business, and she and Tasha had been in two films together. Donna had been discovered as paranormal and had been essentially Morrison's charge since her rescue from the cult.

"Oh, God, it's good," moaned Tasha.

"I love stretching you out like that. You take it, little girl," said Donna gently, not in a dominant fashion.

"Uhhhhhhhhhh," moaned Tasha, about all she could do in the throes of passion.

Suddenly, there was a knock at the door. Donna immediately stopped and said, "Who is it?"

"Sunset. You guys are late."

"Hold on!"

Donna pulled out quickly, producing a yelp from Tasha. They scurried and threw on clothes. Donna wore a black mini-skirt, heels, and a white shirt with blue vertical stripes. Tasha wore a peach colored, long blouse that hung almost entirely over her gray mini-skirt. Her heels were white with pictures of lambs.

"Hurry up," snapped Morgana, who was with her daughter.

Donna opened the door and said, "Uh, sorry!"

Morgana rolled her eyes, leaning on the door frame. Now forty-four, she was tall with long, black hair laced with gray. Her skin was very good, so she either took really good care of it, used a lot of make-up, or was using a glamour. It was the latter. Morgana wore a gold headband and had cat-like, green eyes. She looked sultry and sexy, a witch of modern times. Her figure was tall and thin. She wore black slacks that hugged her hips, a light blue button-down top that had a print of cartoon black cats on it, and black booties. Morgana had tattoos, but they were well hidden under her long, black hair.

"This isn't the time to be literally fucking around," snapped Sunset. About thirty, Sunset had long, wavy light blonde hair that lay halfway down her back, parted not in the middle but towards the left side, yet not completely on the left. Her eyes were a dark brown, wide and sleepy looking. Her jaw was angular and her skin pale, and she appeared to have a gentle, soft look. Her nose was slightly too large for her face, but it as an imperfection that gave her a pretty look. Her eyebrows were painted as such to always be lifted, giving her a perpetually soft, gentle look. When she smiled, she had a mouth a bit larger than proportionate and perfect teeth, so she glowed when she was happy. Today, she wore a black button-down blouse with white roses on it, white pants, and red heels, looking very business professional.

Donna flushed. "Sorry. We're ready."

"Which one of you has the greased-up ass?" asked Morgana with a smirk.

"Me," said Tasha with a flip of her hair. "Let's roll."

"Ah, they have arrived," said Valeria as the four women entered the room.

Connor McLaughlin had arrived as well. The son of Dave McLaughlin, he being a former mentor of Quartet member Amy Dayne, Connor was the leader of this project. Due to his youth, he was aided by long-time Inner Circle member Judge Rodchester Norton, who was now retired and living in the Bahamas. Eighteen-year-old Connor looked like a younger, boyish version of his father. Like Dave, Connor also had fair, blond hair swept to the right, glasses, and a handsome face with sharp blue eyes. But his face was rounder, and his frame lankier like his mother's ostrich-sized shape. He was wearing a yellow dress shirt that wasn't tucked into jeans with white running shoes.

"Let's have a quick status," said Morrison, gesturing them to move in closer. They all gathered around one of several circular lunch tables in the room.

"Okay. We're about to revolutionize the world. We've talked about it, we've done the first phase, and we're ready for phase two. We all know this is a big deal. We all have to be at the top of the game to pull this off. Anyone having any problems?"

Everyone looked around and more or less shrugged or nodded. Valeria was the only one who spoke. "We are eager to complete our transition."

"Right. When we go, this channel takes time. This is a long channel. We've gone through the outline, but I can't emphasize that enough. It's not like flipping on a switch. We stimulate the particles and then they more or less take off on their own . . . sort of like kicking up an old computer and giving it orders then waiting. But once the particles are mixed, once they reach the stimulation point, nothing can stop it." He paused. "And when that happens, the world turns off. No electricity. No power of any kind. Everyone will return to the basics," said Morrison.

"Except us," added Valeria when it was clear Morrison had finished his oratory.

"Yes," said Connor nodding. "All the satellites are set up and we'll continue to operate under 21st century rules here in Glickstenstein."

"Satellites? I don't really get this," said Tasha, looking confused and a lot like the dumb kid in grade school.

"The spell doesn't extend past the Earth's atmosphere, so satellites are unaffected," said Morrison. "In a way, that's fortunate. We don't need them crashing to Earth. They'll operate and eventually flame out."

Connor said, "The Consortium has seventeen satellites to continue monitoring the Earth for weather, disasters, all sorts of things. That includes shooting down other satellites when their orbit finally decays. It's necessary. We must run things until everything stabilizes. And document for history."

"So, we're all staying here because this place will, uh, stay here. Stay as it is now," said Tasha, iterating what she'd heard as she wasn't entirely clear.

"Yep," said Donna with a smile. "You can't run the world hiding in a cave with the cave dwellers. You run it by making sure they're doing the right thing."

"Uh, sure," said Tasha, a little bewildered. She had known only the highest-level outline of the plan. She knew in general terms how it would happen, but she had never really thought of the consequences until now.

"Enough of this banter," snapped Valeria. "We all know our duties once the EMP settles. How fares the tachyon saturation in the atmosphere? When do we go?"

"Soon," said Morrison. "I'm putting it at about mid-afternoon tomorrow."

"Excellent."

Connor stood and said, "It's been an honor to work with all of you. I appreciate your help. The world appreciates it. Myself and Rod, and the rest of the Consortium team, we won't let you down. Once we stop the bleeding, so to speak, and remove all carbon emissions, we can reverse enough of the damage from global warming to save the Earth, normalize it again."

"Yeah, I guess right now, trying that is like bailing out a sinking boat with a sieve," said Morgana.

"True enough," said Valeria. "We should all rest for a time. We will need all of our power tomorrow."

"And what of Ops?" asked Sunset suddenly. "What if they find us first?"

Morrison shrugged. "They won't get down here. If by some miracle they do, they'll die. We can't tolerate interference now. It is victory or death."

Chapter Fifteen
The Golden Age
July 8, 2021

Glickstenstein covered only forty-six square miles, but it was a legitimate force because of Valeria's . . . temperament. The country was the creation of a post-World War II treaty, and its main industry was tourism. The capitol and main city had about forty thousand people. The country as a whole had about fifty thousand people.

The castle sat near a large river with an airstrip in back and a stone bridge over the river in front. The cliff on which the castle rested was very tall. Part of the castle was destroyed in World War II and never rebuilt. There was a stone bridge leading over the river from the main road, the A1, to the building, which was surrounded on the backside by a small airport. About a mile downstream was the docking area for boats for the sea and the tiny village of Puddlestock, while upstream was a factory. The rest of the surrounding area was woodland with some small dirt roads.

The castle was four square towers eight stories tall and eight stories deep around a square courtyard. There were only windows on the first floor of the building. There was a reason for that. This building was called The Alptraum — German for nightmare. This was a prison for Valeria's political prisoners and torture slaves.

The prison held 1,603 prisoners at the time of the spell. Valeria and her team didn't expect any of them to survive. The spell was powered by draining their auras. They would lose their lives and souls, scarified to the greater good.

Such was their penalty for crossing Valeria.

The team had prepared the chamber during the day, breaking only for lunch. A big lunch. This would be a big spell.

The day was the type of hot, muggy rainy day common in summer, with high humidity, a lot of clouds, occasional lightning, and spotty showers and thunderstorms. They would start the spell at four in the afternoon.

The chamber where the spell would be performed was a stone antechamber below the main courtyard. There were no windows, just two doors guarded with iron doors. There were no furnishings in the room, which had stained concrete floors.

Everyone took a few minutes to use the bathroom and otherwise prepare. Tasha ate four candy bars. At four P.M. local time, with the hot sun bright in the sky but storm clouds approaching rapidly, the team entered the basement chamber.

Valeria wore the official dress of her country. This consisted of an olive-green jacket with medals and ribbons, matching pants, a white blouse, and a hat with a red ribbon. She smiled, observing the pentagon laid out on the floor.

"Superb."

She turned and smiled at her four partners, all outside the room. "Welcome to the new world."

Morrison entered, wearing jeans and a white pirate shirt with white Nike sneakers. "Funny, looks like a basement."

Morgana laughed. She wore a black blouse with a black mesh shirt under it and black pants held up by a gold belt. Her shoes were black booties, no heels. "I've been in worse places."

Following her was Sunset, wearing a yellow hoodie with a picture of a smiley face and light-colored blue jeans. Her shoes were flip flops. "Not a day at the beach."

Donna entered, wearing purple yoga pants with white swirls, a yellow blouse that fit loosely, and a smile. "Time to change the world. C'mon, new girl, hurry up."

Tasha was last, being led in by Donna. Tasha wore a brown and white swirled sleeveless shirt and brown pants. "It smells."

None of the women wore any jewelry. That was risky with this spell, due to the possible backlash of psychic heat.

Once they were inside, Valeria closed the door and locked it using an app from her phone. Then she turned and said, "This is not a place of comfort, Tasha. Let us prepare."

At this point, they didn't engage in small talk. They knew there was risk, and they knew the power of the moment. They were about to permanently change the world for the better. They were like Jesus squared.

Morgana frowned. "What are you doing with that thing?" She nodded at Valeria's phone.

Valeria shook her head. "We need the guards in the towers ready in case the prisoners try to escape or rebel as they slowly have their auras drained. They will not be agreeable to this, but that is the fate of those who cross us, to die an ugly death. In their agonies, they will try to escape. Our exterior defenses are reliant on Mr. Morrison's tachyonic inversion spell, that works like an EMP on the aura. But my phone is how I communicate with the guards."

"It's unstoppable," said Morrison.

Sunset nodded. "No one is going to bother us anyhow."

"Y'know, if you're wrong about this, Rhino, you're gonna kill half of the paranormal agents of Special Ops. I guarantee your contract work as a pilot is over," said Sam Grant

Rhino laughed. One of Tripper O'Sullivan's old friends, Rhino was an expert pilot. Now closing in on sixty years old, he had a scruffy blond beard and hair, bright eyes, and a wide smile. He looked a bit like a burned out 1980s version of Gene Hackman, or at least, that's what Tripper always told everyone, and he was right. Medina had secured a military jet for Rhino to pilot.

Radar turned to the rest of the team: Nicole, Medina, Sam, Searly, Thunder, Osa, Tripper, and Ashley. His drone monitoring of activities had worked perfectly, and they knew it was time. The team all wore some manner of black or, in Nicole and Osa's case, dark blue Kevlar. Osa and Nicole also had their longer hair in ponytails.

"Better buckle up, kiddies. You aren't indestructible robots like me," said Radar.

As they buckled in, Tripper said wryly, "I reckon I heard a plane crash can incinerate even the strongest a'metal."

Radar said, "Aw, shut up."

"Peaceful, calm, let it flow into us," said Morrison calmly in the basement of the castle, where the spell had started. "But you cannot lose consciousness. The overwhelming power will hit you, then must be pushed out. Stay calm . . . stay in the moment."

Morrison was in the middle, with the other five of them at five feet apart on the points of the pentagon. Donna was nearest the door, and going to the right were Tasha, Valeria, Sunset, and Morgana. They all stood rigidly precisely on the point. They were all sweating.

"We're already building physic heat," said Sunset calmly but clearly making a warning point.

"It will pass," said Morrison calmly.

They all had their eyes shut, concentrating purely on the control and focus of the aura. They were only minutes away from success, but at this point they were utterly vulnerable.

Rhino's plane landed in the woodlands about a quarter of a mile behind the prison. Instantly, the Ops agents unbuckled and headed for the exit.

Sam said, "The castle is the most secure prison in Europe. They should never have let us land. They must be active in the spell *now* and can't spare any defenses."

"Fuck yeah! Can't you feel it?" asked Radar with alarm.

Nicole said, "It's like my teeth are vibrating."

"Let's move," snapped Sam.

They raced towards the prison, Radar clearing the brush as he was basically a tank and also armed with a flame thrower, Thunder also generating some wind with Ashley and Medina's help. Nicole channeled earth to clear trees and shrubs, aided by Osa.

Nicole pointed. "There!"

They raced along a stairwell that curved around the south side towards the bridge and the main entrance. Radar again had the lead.

There was one security guard at the gate, a pimply faced boy named Lars who had as much chance against the Ops agents as a bee did of flying to Jupiter. Osa knocked him out with wind, blowing him into a wall where he hit his head, as Radar charged the gate.

Then he screamed and froze.

Medina moved forward to help him, but Radar shouted, "No, stay back! *T-t-t-tachyonic EMP!*"

"What do we do?" asked Sam with alarm.

Suddenly, alarms sounded throughout the prison, sounding like tornado sires. That was disconcerting, as was the fact Radar was beginning to vibrate violently, held in place by some unseen force.

"Hold o-onnnnnnnnnnnnnnnn!" he shouted.

There were suddenly sparks and all the Ops agents dove for cover. When they got to their feet, Radar stood there, his outer casing having . . . melted. It had refrozen, so he looked like a wax dummy that had melted.

"Holy shit," gasped Medina.

"Crickey! Are you okay, old man?" asked Thunder.

They were all approaching him slowly, like he was the new kid in school no one was sure about.

Then he said, "I countered it, and caught aural shifts. We're clear. I can move fine. I just look ugly. We've got to get to the room below this place! Now!"

Nicole waved her hands. "Stand back. The only thing that will get through the security and all this concrete in time is a probability skewed earth channel."

They all moved back, Radar a little wobbly, and Nicole stood in the center, staring down at the rock. She focused. . . focused . . . focused . . . then channeled.

And all Hell broke loose.

Nicole's channel ruptured the geometric structure of the pentagon within the prison of squares, and the effect was dramatic.

Like a typhoon, the six Consortium members were sucked out of the antechamber and hurled into the air. Nicole screamed as she was sucked with them.

This completely disrupted the spell. The psychic heat surged through the chamber, but the damage to the building gave it a channel to escape. Exposed to the exterior world, it surged up and out. Moving so fast, no one in the spell was burned. The psychic heat, however, killed a handful of prison officials working in an office on the first floor.

Following the ejection of Morrison's team was the ejection of a fountain of water and mud as the Consortium team had been drawing on the river as the cooling source for the spell. That all flowed from under the prison out, and the courtyard was almost completely secured. There was no outlet, other than the small area by the main gate.

"*Hold on!*" shrieked Medina as the courtyard was inundated in water and mud that was like a flash flood.

Ashley grabbed Sam and said, "Hang on!"

"Help!" shouted Searly, unable to channel water and earth.

Tripper grabbed her, and like surfers, they held on through the violence, being swept towards the west prison building. "Hold on, McTaggert! This ain't gonna be easy!"

The result of the chaotic semi-tidal wave was to separate everyone. Morrison also found himself near the door of the west prison building, and he ran inside.

"Sam!" shouted Searly, coughing up water as she and Tripper crashed into the wall.

Sam ran towards them, the water rapidly subsiding, leaking out through doors and primarily the main gate. The sound had been deafening, but it had lowered now as well, enabling Sam to hear Searly's cry.

Tripper hit hard and broke his cane on the impact. He cursed as he slammed his knee into the wall. Searly hit hard, but mostly on her shoulder, and was relatively okay.

Sam raced forward and helped her up. "You okay?"

She nodded and said, "Let's get these dirtbags."

Turning to Tripper, Sam said, "C'mon, old timer."

"I'm a'comin'," said Tripper, using the lower half of his cane to get to his feet. "God damn, I've had this cane longer than I can remember. It's like someone shot my dog."

"I'll buy you a new one," said Sam.

They took off after Morrison. The prison corridor was concrete block painted white with barricades every twenty yards. There were gray doors to the side numbered with large stencil numbers painted in black on the doors. There were no windows. Based on how close together the doors were, the rooms were very small.

Morrison raced through the barriers, which were some type of shatterproof plastic, using a palm reader to gain entry. He slammed them shut behind him.

Tripper had no problem rupturing them with a focused earth channel. He was moving behind Sam and Searly.

They chased Morrison through three such barriers, by which point Morrison was huffing and puffing. Not only was the run exhausting, but the spell had been tiring as well. Finally, he had reached a T-intersection he sought, and he went to the right.

Sam, Searly, and Tripper couldn't catch him because they needed a couple of seconds to clear the barrier each time. He had also used TK to fling the debris from the doors back at them, but Searly easily melted the plastic pieces. Her lighter had been in her boots and hadn't gotten wet.

As they neared the intersection, Searly got in the lead, ahead of wounded Tripper and arthritic Sam. She paused at the corner and slid to the ground, then peeked around the corner.

But Morrison was ready, and he grabbed her by the hair and channeled his unique emotional channeling ability into her. Because of his NDE, he could call upon the images of the dead.

For Searly, the attack was abrupt, instant, and overwhelming. One second she was in the hallway, and the next she was watching Clarke die, strangled by Quafara in the battle in Atlantia.[21]

"Searly!" shouted Sam, hearing her God-awful wail of despair. When Sam had joined Ops in '07, Searly was one of the first agents he met. They were more than co-workers, they were friends, and they had been through an awful lot of death together: Clarke, Bam, Meredith, just for starters. If there was one person Sam could not handle suffering pain, it was Searly.

Enraged, he dove at Morrison and hit him hard, driving him backwards with a flying tackle worthy of an NFL linebacker, no mean feat for an arthritic man in his fifties. Rage and adrenaline fueled him.

The flying tackle knocked Morrison backwards into the wall. "Get off, you nut!" he shouted, grabbing Sam by the shirt and flinging him down the hallway. Then Morrison channeled earth and drove Sam away, burying him in tile, concrete and debris.

But by now, Tripper had caught up. He paused, seeing Searly lying unconscious on the floor, disturbingly white. But he had to take down Morrison before he could help her. Pointing with his remaining half of his cane, he said, "Y'all is one dead sumbitch if'n y'all hurt that girl."

"God, can't you fucking people leave us alone! We're trying to save the world!"

"Hitler said the same shit," said Tripper.

They both channeled air and earth, and it was a standoff. But Morrison got a hand on Tripper's leg and tried to use his emotional channeling.

Tripper stomped on Morrison's head and hit him with the cane like a clean-up hitter in baseball going for a grand slam. That knocked Morrison down the hallway, blood flying from the side of his face and nose.

---

[21] In 2015, as seen in TM 1.13 "The Mind of the Gods"

"Y'all can't use that shit on me. Back in the day, the Trouts imbued me with enough zombie magic to offset that NDE shit you use."

Tripper moved in for the kill, but he was an old man, ungainly in the best of times, and working with a badly bruised and swollen knee. He stumbled a little, and that gave Morrison a chance to swing his right leg up and kick Tripper in the balls. Hard.

Tripper gasped and stumbled back, allowing Morrison to gain full control of a wind channel and drive him back down the hallway, past the T-intersection. That shoved him into the first plastic barrier, and he hit it like a bug on a windshield. That dropped him unconscious to the floor.

Morrison turned and ran the other way, past Sam, who was coming around. All Morrison wanted to do was get his ass back to LA. He had no interest in killing anyone.

Sam heard him leave as he dug his way out of debris, shirt ripped and his face and arms and hands badly cut. He had three deep cuts on his right arm.

"Fuck," he muttered. "This shit never happens to Captain America."

Suddenly, he saw Searly on her back.

She was not breathing.

Sam couldn't have chased Morrison anyhow, because he'd broken his leg, though he didn't know it yet. His right shin was fractured. It hurt, but he thought it was a bruise. He stumbled to Searly and horrified realized she was already starting to turn a tinge of blue.

She was not breathing. He checked her pulse.

Nothing.

"God damn!" he shouted, and he immediately started CPR. He could see Tripper was down the hall not moving, but he was breathing.

Sam didn't even pray. He didn't have time. He had to get her breathing again.

Suddenly, she had a heartbeat.

"Fuck! Thank you, God, for small favors."

However, as Sam looked around, he realized something horrible. The collapsing structure had barricaded them inside. Morrison had fled out a tunnel that was now flooding, and with Tripper unconscious, Sam had no way to get them out.

He might have saved Searly's life only to die with her.

Chapter Sixteen
Revenge

"My God, I'm going to kill you two so fucking dead they won't even be able to find you in Hell," hissed Nicole.

Nicole, Sunset, and Morgana had landed hard in a conference room that was secure against external assault. The room was about eight hundred square feet with a large table in the middle, computers and screens along the walls, and only a single door. The door had been open, so the water rushed in and swept the three women inside. Sunset and Morgana used channeling to direct themselves, but the water was too powerful and swept them into the far side of the room, where they hit the wall. Nicole had more control and had the wave drop her at the door. She channeled hard for a moment to stop the wave, then slammed the door shut and locked the door.

Nicole raised her hands as she hissed her threat, and Sunset and Morgana raised theirs.

But something odd happened.

When the door shut, the room, which was a square, suddenly became a bizarre force of geometric channeling that was full of the tachyonic discharge from Morrison's spell. They were in water up to their knees, so psychic heat wasn't an issue.

What was an issue was their ability to channel. It suddenly stopped.

"What the fuck?" said Nicole.

All three of them had their hands out and suddenly realized channeling was inaccessible in the room.

Morgana snapped at Sunset, "We must be in one of the antechambers and the square shape is holding particles from the spell."

"Who fucking cares, mother?" whined Sunset.

Nicole had figured this out as well. She pulled off her belt and began wrapping it around her right fist as she said, "Well, every time we've fought, it was two against one. In terms of power, I couldn't match that. You killed my father, you made me kill, you tried to kill thousands for some retarded plan. But it's over now, because now, sure, it's two against one. But I can fight. And you," she said with a nod to Sunset, "are a big pussy and you," and she nodded at Morgana, "are an old bitch."

"Fuck you," said Sunset, but she looked scared and was shrinking to the corner.

Morgana grimaced and took a step forward. "We'll see, Smith. All you've ever done is talk."

The room had only the central table and a lot of water as a barrier. There was nowhere to run or hide. All three women knew this was the end, one way or the other.

Morgana moved to attack Nicole, protecting her daughter.

Nicole was ready. When Morgana jumped to the table to jump on Nicole, Nicole quickly kicked out and knocked Morgana's legs from under her. As Morgana fell, Nicole hit her in the side of the face with a roundabout left and knocked her into the water.

Moving fast, Nicole came after Sunset, who was defending the corner to limit Nicole to a direct attack. Sunset was not a fighter. She'd always used her channeling power and always worked from a perspective of dominance. Being trapped with Nicole, who was babbling incoherently and clearly furious, Sunset didn't know what to do.

She feebly kicked out, but the water slowed her kick so much that Nicole caught Sunset's right leg and pulled it, causing Sunset to fall back into the water.

Morgana had not gotten up. She was under the water line.

Sunset screamed, then was silent as Nicole pulled Sunset's legs out from under her and caused Sunset to fall fully under the water line. Nicole then jumped on top of her and pinned her with her knees on Sunset's shoulders.

Horrified, Sunset realized she was drowning.

Nicole didn't like this position. Her back was to Morgana, so if Morgana recovered, Nicole was vulnerable.

But Nicole didn't care and wasn't moving. She sure as shit was going to make sure Sunset died.

Even though she knew Sunset couldn't hear her, Nicole hissed, "This is for my father, you slut. This is for Tabitha. This is for everyone you and your whore life have fucked up. I hope it hurts."

Nicole's head was pounding, and she was seeing red as she murdered Sunset. And she was not letting up.

For an eternity, she sat on the writhing struggling Sunset who had no chance of dislodging Nicole. Sunset grew weaker every second. She tried to get her hands up to attack Nicole, but with her shoulders pinned, she could only flail helplessly as she was drowned.

Sunset's struggles grew slower.

Nicole sat on her.

Sunset stopped moving.

Nicole sat on her.

Finally . . . Nicole counted to one-eighty, three minutes, and then stood up.

Sunset didn't move.

Nicole went to find Morgana. She pulled Morgana out of the water and realized she was dead as well, a huge welt on her head. She'd hit something when she fell into the water, lost consciousness, and drowned.

Nicole slapped Morgana's corpse's face and said, "I hope it hurt, you disgusting, filthy, cum-bucket whore."

Then she heaved Sunset's body to the table as well. Sunset was clearly dead as well.

"I did it," gasped Nicole.

She looked to the heavens. "I'm sorry it took so long, father. And I'm sorry I had to do it this way, but they were too dangerous to live."

A statement that was true, but only partially. Because Nicole had really, truly wanted to kill them. She wanted her revenge . . . *needed* her revenge.

For several minutes, Nicole just sat on the table, breathing hard, and stared at the corpses of the two people she hated the most, the two people that for years had tormented her and caused her pain, that had irrevocably shattered her life. It felt good knowing it was over.

She felt free.

She felt no regret whatsoever.

This was not like when she killed Tabitha. Sunset and Morgana had killed dozens, if not hundreds, and would have killed billions. The world had no place for them.

Finally, reality set in. She realized she was stuck inside the room and possibly the corridor outside was full of water. If she opened the door, she'd be able to channel, but if the water was too strong, she could get swept back inside and drown.

Then she heard an odd noise, like the whoosh of a vacuum cleaner. Someone was clearing the corridor of water.

Nicole raced to the door and opened it, ready for battle.

But it was Medina.

Medina turned to her right and said with happy surprise, "Nicole! You're okay!"

"I am."

They hugged, and Medina knew whatever happened had been serious.

"It's . . . it's over."

"Over?" asked Medina as they broke the ug.

"Sunset, Morgana and I were swept in here. I was able to channel and keep my head above water and avoid hitting anything. They . . . they didn't. Morgana went under, then Sunset did as well. I was too busy taking care of myself to help them." She nodded back. "Bodies are in there."

Medina gave Nicole a hard look, which Nicole met. They said nothing for a time. Then Medina quickly said, "Okay, let's go. Let's get out of here. I have no idea who is okay and who isn't without coms."

"Did we stop the spell?"

"Oh, yes. But as long as any of these guys are loose, I think we're in danger."

Chapter Seventeen
The Last Stand

Valeria was hurled towards the rear exit, which were two steel security double-doors that led to an airstrip behind the prison. The force of the water blew the doors off their hinges, and water flowed outside and flooded the patio and steps which led to the doors, the red and yellow flags of Glickstenstein posted in holders on each side. Past that was a small grassy median, then a dirt road, then three runways for small to mid-sized planes. There were two aircraft hangers, one to the right and the other across the field, and three big, blue trash dumpsters.

Lightning danced in the distance and the sun had vanished. There was a humid mist in the air. Storms were imminent.

Valeria landed just inside the double doors and looked around. She had no idea where everyone had gone, so decided the best approach was to get outside and get into a plane. Airborne, she could assess the situation.

Or run.

However, Ashley and Thunder had also been driven in this direction, and they had exited *first*, unknown to Valeria. Thunder ducked behind one of the dumpsters, trying to get it together, a little groggy from being swept along the walls like a piece of trash in a flash flood. He'd been bounced around more than Ashley, who was a stronger water channeler and used the flood to direct their wash outside and to at least temporary safety.

While Thunder got it together and covered Ashley, she looked around. There was a large red and yellow plane on the closest runway, Valeria's personal aircraft. Ashley headed for the plane. The stairs leading to the airplane's door were down, standard emergency protocol. Ashley raced aboard.

Inside, it was a magnificent and expensive, all in the red and yellow colors of the country of Glickstenstein.

Ashley whistled and said to herself, "Damn, it looks like something from James Bond."

The plane was empty, so she turned and raced won the stairs. As she hit the runway, she froze, for Valeria exited the prison at that moment.

Striking a stewardess pose, Ashley said, "Sorry, ma'am, but the flight is overbooked."

Valeria jutted her jaw forward in the preening, arrogant manner she always displayed when challenged and said, "I would prefer not to hurt you, woman."

Ashley glared. "Considerate. But it's hard to take you at your word since, you know, ohhhhhhh, well, when you took over your postage-stamp country you decapitated all the council officials and stuck their heads on pikes outside the palace."

"I was a younger much more foolish woman then. More emotional. They were criminals and I wanted to make an example . . . I was only fifteen."

Ashley was biding time, building power, but she had no desire whatsoever to fight Valeria. She knew from Ops' files Valeria was in the top of the class. Ashley was strong herself, but a pitched battle between them was, at best, a 50/50 proposition. She was just biding time for Thunder to ambush Valeria.

Thunder did so, bringing down the distant lightning while also racing forward and diving at Valeria.

Unfortunately, Valeria easily dodged Thunder's attempt at a tackle and channeled the dumpster in front of her, which drew the lightning strike.

"Crickey!" shouted Thunder, moving to channel more lightning from the rapidly approaching thunderstorm.

Ashley charged forward, shouting, "Death to Glickstenstein!" All she wanted to do was draw Valeria's attention so Thunder could bring down the electric hammer, so to speak.

Using TK, Valeria hurled some of the flagpoles at Ashley.

Thunder focused the lightning.

Ashely slowed the flags, which had protruding points, as they approached her. She dodged two and caught one in her right hand.

Lightning flashed towards Valeria.

So did Ashley. The poles were PVC pipe, not metal, so she wasn't worried about drawing the lightning, especially give Thunder was channeling it.

Valeria dove to the right to dodge the lightning, landing on the grass and rolling on her back.

She was wide open.

Ashley shouted and drove the point of the flagpole into Valeria's chest, both of them screaming as Valeria was skewered and pinned to the ground like a bug under the penetration of a penknife.

Valeria screamed for only a few seconds.

And then she died.

Ashley had penetrated her heart.

Ashley gasped and leaned on the pole. Valeria was clearly dead, her eyes wide and unmoving.

"Jesus Criminey," said Thunder, coming over and moving her from the pole.

"Queen of nothing," said Ashley, spitting on Valeria's corpse.

"Easy, sheila, easy," said Thunder gently.

Suddenly a little shocked, Ashley looked up at him and said, "She's . . . whoa, she's dead."

"Yeah."

"I . . . I just killed her."

"It's okay. Keep it together. This isn't over. We've got to find the others."

"But . . . I killed her."

He held her. "I know. We'll talk later. But our friends need us now, and so does the world, I'd guess."

Ashley nodded, took a final look at the corpse, and raced after Thunder towards a walkway that would lead to the front of the castle.

Out front, Osa and melted Radar had landed hard against the front gate. The floodwaters and debris hurled them out the front gate, depositing them on the bridge. Behind them came Donna and Tasha.

Radar recovered first, of course. He was a few yards from Tasha and blasted her with a sonic wave.

Osa struggled to get to her feet. Donna was crying and used TM telekinesis to hurl bricks and pieces of the castle at Osa.

"Owwww!" yelped Osa as bricks hit her hard. Osa rolled to her left, putting her near the edge of the bridge, which was dangerous as the guard rail had collapsed and the river below was moving fast due to heavy rain already falling up in the mountains. Thunder rumbled as she balanced.

Osa countered, sending an earth channel at Donna and causing her to fall back as Osa shouted, "This is not the Middle Ages! Stoning is illegal!"

Radar quickly pulled a syringe from his belt and knocked out Tasha, who lay on the ground wailing in pain with her hands over her ears. Once he had done that, he caught Donna. Donna and Tasha weren't fighters, so Radar had no problem injecting either.

Then he looked at Osa. "What happened in there? Where are the others?"

"I don't know. Can't you read them?" asked Osa worriedly.

"Something inside is blocking me," he shouted over a very strong rumble of thunder.

Before he could say anything else, a bolt of lightning struck down from the sky. Osa yelped and threw her hands over her face, almost blinded.

When it cleared, Radar stood smoking on the bridge, his Kevlar having burned off.

"Radar?" asked Osa in horror.

Rain started pouring down.

"Shit," she muttered, realizing he must have been knocked offline by the lightning. She knew he wasn't dead. But he also couldn't help her.

She headed for the gate, deciding to move inside to find the others and get out of the storm. Just as she was about to go inside, Morrison suddenly appeared.

Osa threw up her hands and tried to blow him away, but he was slightly faster and threw a boulder her way.

The result was that she blew him into a wall and knocked him out. However, she was too close to the edge of the bridge, and it began to collapse from the impact.

"Oh, fuck!" she shouted, realizing she was falling into the river.

She angled and managed a reasonable dive and avoided other falling rock and stone.

Radar fell into the river as well, or at least the smoking metal that was all that was left of this particular robotic version of him. Osa ignored that. Once she hit the water, she focused on avoiding debris and getting to shore. The river was moving fast with water from the storm further upstream, so she was swept downstream about a half a mile before she was able to fight the current and use water channeling to get a wave to dump her on the shore. She landed on a sandy inlet with a lot of trash.

Rolling onto her back, she gasped for air and was grateful she was alive.

"Whoa, are they dead?" asked Nicole of Medina as they finally reached the front gate and found Donna and Tasha lying in the debris.

Medina quickly checked and said, "No, out cold, I think one of our team drugged them."

"Oh, shit. The bridge has partially collapsed. You think they went under?"

Medina looked to her right — and saw Osa moving slowly on the inlet. Pointing, she said to Nicole, "I see Osa!"

Nicole turned to look.

At that moment, Morrison, who had regained consciousness, made his move. He was desperate to escape. He channeled his death-experience tachyonic force into both women. They both screamed and felt to the ground and started rolling around.

He saw a police car nearby that had keys and more importantly hadn't been damaged. He jumped into it and started to race away on the bridge.

Nicole was devastated by the blast. She suddenly was falling from a skyscraper endlessly, unable to fly or hit bottom, replaying the trauma of her initial manifestation of channeling when her father's old agent and TM Helena had thrown Nicole off a building in Anaheim.

But Medina dealt with her trauma. She knew it well, and as it hit, she realized it was an attack. Writing on the ground, she escaped the nightmare and channeled earth with all she had, for she had only a second or two before Morrison was out of range.

She won.

Her channel caused the bridge to finally give way.

They all went down.

"Oh, fuckkkkkkkkkkkkkk meeeeeeeeeee!" shouted Medina.

Nicole snapped out of it and realized she really *was* falling. They both desperately channeled wind to blunt their fall, then channeled water in the river.

Morrison landed in the car and one of the support beams and major boulders of the bridge landed right on top of the car, crushing him like a bug.

The two women channeled water and rode out the rush. They angled and brought themselves ashore near Osa, Nicole by far suffering the most, having taken on a lot of water.

Osa helped Nicole to her knees as she coughed out river water. Medina breathed deeply and said, "That was exhausting!"

"You did great, though!" shouted Osa like a sorority girl winning a major prize.

Medina pointed to the castle. "We know Morrison died in the river. I saw the car get crushed. Donna and Tasha were up there unconscious. Any news on the others?"

Nicole looked up and saw movement in the brush. She tried to cry out, but water caught, and she coughed violently.

Then Ashley and Thunder came through the brush as thunder rumbled. Ashley said, "This is no time for a beach party, ladies!"

"Ash! Bogut!" shouted Medina, racing for them. "Thank God you're okay."

"Valeria is dead," said Thunder. "The three of us wound up in the airfield and she didn't want to pay the flight tax."

"Good . . . riddance," muttered Nicole, finally able to talk. "Sunset and Morgana are dead."

"Who's left?" asked Osa.

Medina quickly said, "None of their team. They're dead, except for Donna and Tasha who are up top unconscious."

Nicole's eyes suddenly widened, and she grabbed Medina. "Boss! The bridge collapsed. They may not be up there any more."

"Come on," said Medina, leading the way along the shore of the river. Most of the area along it was foliage and trash, but so much of the bridge had landed and swept that now it was more like a rocky path. AS a result, despite the urgency, they had to move carefully.

"Anyone seen the old men and Searly?" asked Osa.

"Nope. I bet they're still inside," said Thunder.

"Shit," said Nicole.

As they neared the cliffside that had previously anchored the bridge, they found Donna's body, her back clearly broken in a fall. And just a bit further upstream was Tasha, face down in the water, dead as well, likely drowned.

Medina said grimly, "I'm sorry they died, but they created their own demise."

Nicole looked at the cliffside and said, "We're not climbing up there."

"We can't waste time. The others must need our help," said Ashley urgently.

Suddenly, the castle intercom activated, and they heard the unmistakable voice of Mister Sam Grant.

"Good afternoon. I regret to inform you this prison is now under American control. Your cells are secure. Please do not panic. We will be assisting an evacuation shortly." He paused as thunder rumbled. "Will any Ops agents please report to the control room? I've deactivated the aural blocker and Tripper has cleared the tachyonic surge. We don't sense any hostile auras. Oh, and Searly says hi. The crisis is over."

The women whopped and Thunder chuckled.

"Aw, fuck. This still leaves a problem," said Nicole suddenly.

"What?" asked Osa alarmed.

She pointed. "Now we have to walk our tired, sorry asses around the back and uphill to get inside."

Medina laughed. "Your ass is fat. A walk will do you good."

They all laughed at that.

"Reckon we did it, McTaggert!" said Tripper, giving her a high-five as they stood in the control room. There were no lights, except for the lights from the monitoring screens.

"I'm glad," she said, smiling, but clearly upset about the memory of Clarke's death.

Sam was running things, but he paused and said to her, "You okay?"

"He hurt me." She paused, angry. "But I'll be okay. Clarke was a great man . . . you know that. I won't let Morrison cheapen his memory."

Sam nodded, knowing they needed to talk more later. He figured the same would be true of Ashley. Sam was quickly establishing contact with the WSA and United Nations to assure a smooth transition of power, given Thunder's call that Valeria was dead.

"We're a gonna have a lotta explain' to do on this one," said Tripper, rubbin' his beard. "At least I woke up in time to get us outta that sump hole!"

"Yeah, I'm glad. That place was gross," said Searly. They were both watching Sam over his shoulder.

"Sorry about your cane, old man," said Sam.

"Ahhhhhhhhh, it can be fixed. It's just a right damn pain in the keister. I got me a lotta other shit to do." He nodded. "I'm just glad we stopped them and none of us got killed. That's what counts. We saved millions of lives today. I can trade m'cane for that."

"You said it, Trip," said Searly.

"That's easy for you two to say," moaned Sam. "I'm going to be stuck here with Medina sorting out the politics of Glickstenstein's transition for the rest of my fucking life!"

Epilogue
The Men in the Room

"I suppose you're here to kill me," said Connor to the darkness behind him.

There was no immediate answer, just the sound of tennis shoes on tile. Connor was in the server room in the government headquarters about a mile from the castle. He was reviewing the battle, still grieving over the loss of his friends and the collapse of their plan three days ago . . . the collapse of an empire.

An empire he was now in charge of.

A light turned on. The server room was cold and sterile, full of computers and servers along the wall with an island that had eight laptops for manual entry before it. Connor sat at one of these workstations, wearing a gray hoodie and jeans, looking like a depressed teenager, which he was.

The light wasn't bright. But it was right enough to reveal Little Jack McGrath and his two sisters, Lisa and Sherry.

"No. Buck up, McLaughlin. I'm actually here to help you save the world," said Little Jack without his normal smile.

Connor looked at him with confusion and annoyance. "If this is a trick, don't bother. If you're strong enough to break through the defenses, there's nothing I can do to stop you from killing me."

Little Jack sat in the workstation next to Connor. "No, son. No. Connor, as I said, we're here to save the world. You know of my sisters?"

"Of course. Consortium intel is the best . . . they're quite lovely for being dead."

"We were freed from Hell thanks to Little Jack," said Lisa.

Sherry added, "We *are* here to help."

Connor shrugged. "I seem to be as big a failure as my father and Calico, so I'm listening."

Little Jack leaned forward with his elbows on his knees and rubbed his hands together, then said, "Last year, I had a discussion with Calico in Germany, meant merely as a distraction, but it grew into something more." He paused. "Back in '18, I was split across all dimensions. All the events in all the dimensions hit me, but they were completely mixed up and without context. Imagine watching a weekend of NFL games with all the plays randomly thrown together."

"Confusing."

"Yes. But as time passed, the context began to clear. I told Calico in that meeting that in every world, humanity survives." He paused and looked Connor in the eyes. "But it survives *best* when *you and I work together.*"

"Best?"

"The conflicts in the world now will have great cost. All deals cost something. The deal now is for you and I — and by I, I mean the McGrath Group — to save this place."

"Why now?" asked Connor.

"Your EMP plan failed to create a Golden Age, but that's not all bad. That plan had serious risks. And the tachyonic discharge has profound implications on the natural tachyons in the atmosphere. It's made the atmosphere charged, to use a simple term, and ripe for new possibilities that *didn't* exist before."

Connor was starting to listen, sensing hope and opportunity. Having never failed at anything and been pampered by the Society most of his life, he had been unprepared for the Golden Age plan to fail and couldn't deal with it. Like his father, Connor had a bit of ego in him. "Possibilities?"

Little Jack smiled his salesman smile, which was always a winner. "All we need . . . all we need is a tachyon well. And, well, a couple other small things. The key is, now that the atmosphere is charged, with a little work from the science team, we'll be able to truly fix global warming."

"Forever?"

Little Jack laughed. "Well, as long as it matters. I mean, the shelf life would be longer than the Earth will last, which is another problem. It really *will* be a Golden Age."

Connor was stunned. But he was still cautious. "Is this an Ops mission?"

"No," said Sherry quickly. "The McGrath group detached from Ops when we formed a few months ago."

Little Jack quickly added, "We're a good team. Me, Joy. My sisters, redeemed from Hell. Well, and a talking, serial killer penguin. Fred. Him I'm not sure about yet."

Connor ignored that. "So, McGraths and Ops are no longer associated?"

Little Jack smiled. "We never were. And you know that. I know you're smart enough and careful enough to know that."

Connor nodded. "I just wanted to see if you'd be honest."

"Hey, we're honest. This goes beyond organizations and borders, beyond loyalty and betrayal, beyond most things, Connor. This is saving the Earth in a way that is perfect and won't harm anyone. Not a *single* person."

"No one?"

"Not directly," said Little Jack with a sudden frown. "But like Ops, like everyone else with power in this game, this much power in the hands of one person is bound to create . . . conflict. We can't control that. If they can't behave, they get slapped. This is more important."

Connor mulled this over. He was stunned, but it was certainly worth listening to because, after all, he had no better options.

He looked at Lisa, then Sherry, then Little Jack and said, "Well . . . I'm in. What do we do?"

Little Jack clapped his hands. "We get to work."